Forgiving Flynn

Falling for You | Book 2

A.M. Olenick

Scarlet Lantern Publishing

Chapter 1

Delaney

N orth Shore is a small, picturesque lake town in Upstate New York. Located about thirty minutes from Syracuse, North Shore offers many amenities year round. In the summer, it's a major tourist destination because of the lake activities and the many festivals the town has from May through September. It's also just as busy in the fall because of fall foliage tours, pumpkin picking, the Halloween parade, and trick-or-treating.

In winter months, there is the yearly town-wide house decorating contest, tree lighting, Christmas parade, and the annual Christmas Festival that runs from mid-December until Christmas Eve. And then, every New Year's Eve, there's a huge blowout party at Town Hall. Spring tends to be quiet in North Shore, but there are still things to be done once the flowers begin to bloom.

My brother and I were born and raised in North Shore, and we attended just about every fair, festival, tree lighting, and parade while we were growing up. We were townies, and as we grew up, I couldn't picture living anywhere else. It's where my family and friends were. It's where I landed my dream job. And it's where I decided I would raise my family—if I was ever blessed with the chance to have one.

"So, are you looking forward to your date tomorrow night?" my best friend, Joy, asks me.

Oh, crap. That's right.

"Uh, yes and no . . . " I reply.

I've never been one for blind dates, but even I have to admit that my luck in the dating department is absolutely terrible. I've been single for quite a while now and was nervous when Joy suggested it, but what could a blind date hurt?

"Why yes, and why no?"

"I don't know. I just feel very uncomfortable about the whole thing . . . not knowing the dude. But I know I need to live outside of my comfort zone a little, and you know him, so I'll give it a go."

"Good. You're going to like Bryant, I think. He's smart, nice, and handsome. I think it'll go well."

"I hope so."

I might not necessarily be confident in the whole blind date thing, but Joy definitely has good taste in men. She landed Jason Williams years ago, and every woman in town was jealous, except for me. I was super excited for my bestie.

I glance out the coffee shop window and admire the town. My town. It's been so freaking cold lately and today is no exception. Plus, there is snow everywhere. A recent storm dumped over twenty inches of snow on us in the span of two days. Daytime temperatures haven't reached higher than maybe twenty degrees in well over a month. It's been one of the coldest winters I can remember, and I should be miserable, but I've lived here for so long that I'm actually used to the cold and snow.

"What are your plans for today?" Joy asks.

"I was planning to go by the B&B for a little bit, then head home and relax. How about you?"

"I have to go shopping for last-minute Christmas presents. I was going to ask if you wanted to come with me, but I guess that would be a no. I should have known better," Joy replies, rolling her eyes.

I can't believe Christmas is next week. I've been somewhat of a workaholic since Mom and Dad gave me more responsibility at the B&B, and

I've always worked the holidays, so being off this year feels super strange. I'm not sure I know how to enjoy a holiday off anymore. Joy has tried time and time again to get me to take a step back and enjoy life a little bit, but it's easy to stay at work for extra hours when you don't have anyone to go home to. Plus, Mom and Dad aren't getting any younger. I'm sure they're getting closer to wanting to retire and I want to make sure that they know the B&B will be in good hands. Amazing hands, actually.

"I would, but I want to stop by and make sure everything is all set for the Christmas Eve dinner."

"Aren't you on vacation?"

"Well, yes, but . . . " I begin.

"But nothing. John knows the Christmas Eve dinner like the back of his hand. I mean, you trained him. I'm sure he can handle it."

"Yes, I trained him, but this is the first year in a long time that I'm actually off for Christmas. I kind of hate it."

True story.

"Go home, Del! Or come do some shopping with me. I'll help take your mind off work. I promise."

I don't doubt for a second that Joy would be able to help keep my mind off work, but I'm just feeling really blah about not being there. Yes, it's a job, but the B&B is so much more than just a job to me. And to my family. It's our business and the people that stay with us become our friends and extended family. It's super weird to not be there this year.

"I don't know. Maybe," I reply, even though I know I'm going to stop at the B&B.

"You're going to stop there, aren't you?"

I don't have to answer; my face says it all.

"You're hopeless, Del!"

Joy and I both laugh, then continue drinking our coffees. I'm facing the door, so I'm the first one who sees him walk into the coffee shop. He walks toward the line at the counter and then stops. My arms break out in goosebumps and the little hairs on the back of my neck stand up.

Oh my god.

The most drop-dead gorgeous man I've ever seen just walked into the coffee shop, and he is standing a few feet from my table. He has to be at least six feet tall, probably more. He has dark hair and dark eyes, though I can't tell the exact color from here. I do know one thing for sure, though. He is absolutely gorgeous! His eyes find mine almost immediately, and I quickly look away. I know he caught me gawking, and I instantly feel my cheeks begin to heat.

Great.

My face must say loads because Joy puts her cup down and stares at me. "Del . . . are you okay?" she asks, concerned.

"Uh, I'm fine. Yeah. Great. Why?"

"Because your face is bright red, and you look like a deer in headlights right now. What's up?"

"Whatever you do, do not turn around. Got it?"

"Yes. Why?"

"The sexiest man I think I've ever seen just walked in and is standing at the back of the line," I whisper.

Joy leans forward. "Have we seen him before? Is he a local?"

I glance at him, then quickly look away before he sees me staring at him again.

"He looks familiar, but I'm not sure to be honest."

The line for the counter finally moves up enough so the handsome stranger is standing parallel to our table. Joy nonchalantly glances to the side and checks him out. Then she looks back at me with wide eyes.

"Oh my god," she whispers.

"I know, right?"

We don't really say anything else. We just sip our coffee and give each other looks. To outsiders, it may look odd, but Joy and I have had our own facial expression language for years. We never seem to need words to know what the other is thinking, and this occasion is no exception. The line moves up, then moves up again and now the handsome stranger is standing behind me. A minute or two later I hear him order his coffee and I swear, I've slipped into a dreamworld. A world where this tall, gorgeous stranger with an incredibly deep, sexy voice takes me away and does unthinkable things to me.

I'm about to say something when I see someone walk up to our table out of the corner of my eye. Joy and I both look up at the same time, and I'm pretty sure I must look like a crazy deer in headlights again.

"Excuse me, ladies, I'm sorry to interrupt. Can you please tell me where Lakeview Drive is?"

The question is spoken to both of us, but the handsome stranger's eyes haven't left mine since he walked up to the table and I looked up at him. I want to respond, but I can't seem to find words of any kind. None. I must look like a complete and total idiot right now. Thankfully Joy must sense my absolute panic because she clears her throat, which takes the stranger's eyes off me.

"Yes. Make a left out of the coffee shop, walk three blocks, then make a right. That's Lakeview Drive."

"Thank you so much," Mister Handsome says.

"You're welcome," Joy replies.

I kind of feel invisible right now, and its my own fault. I couldn't find my voice and he probably thinks I'm a weirdo now.

I'm looking at Joy when I feel eyes on me again. I look up and see that he's looking at me again.

My god, is he gorgeous.

His stare is so incredibly intense, and I feel like my heart is going to pound right out of my chest. We are locked in a staring contest for a few more seconds before Handsome blinks a few times then looks away.

"Anyway, have a lovely day, ladies," he says.

I nod, then realize a nod is a shitty response, so I clear my throat and attempt to speak without making myself look like more of an ass.

"Thank you. You too."

Tall and Handsome nods and smiles, then walks out of the coffee shop.

"Who the hell was that?" Joy asks loudly.

"I have *no* idea, but my god, is he sexy!"

"Definitely. You're lucky I'm not single, or I'd be after that too."

"Oh please. He was just being nice. Tall, sexy men like that don't go for curvy women like me."

Joy gives me a look, and I know she would probably smack me if we weren't in public right now.

"I know. I know," I reply, raising my hands in surrender.

"Good. Because I don't want to have to smack you every time you say something negative about yourself. *But* I will."

I've been curvy my entire life, and I've never been ashamed of how I look. Where other girls usually wear single digit sizes, I've been a very comfortable size fourteen for years, and I've never wanted to be any less. But guys never seem to even look at me, let alone want to be with me. I've been single for so long now and it's really taken a toll on my confidence.

Joy and I finish up our coffees, then bundle up so we can head back out into the frozen tundra that is our home.

"What are you going to wear tomorrow, Del?" Joy asks as we make our way down the sidewalk.

"I don't know. Pants, a sweater, and boots?"

Joy stops walking and gives me another one of her famous looks.

"Oh, come on, Joy. It's freezing and slippery!"

"I don't care. You are going to dress up for this date. You guys are going to hit it off, and then we can double date!"

We start walking again and I turn my head so Joy doesn't see me roll my eyes. There is a fat chance that this date is going to go well, but I am going to see it through because Joy is my best friend, and I haven't been on a date in years.

"Okay, well, thank you for walking me to the store. Have fun checking in at the B&B," Joy says, rolling her eyes.

"Don't sass me. I just have to make sure—"

"Yeah, yeah. Love you," Joy says, pulling open the door to the store.

"Love you too," I reply before I walk off.

One of the great things about North Shore is that pretty much anything of importance is located relatively close to the center of town. That includes my work, Joy's work, the bank, the store, at least three doctor's offices, multiple restaurants, and—the most important to me—my house. A few minutes after I leave Joy at the store, I arrive at my family's bed and breakfast. I push the door open and walk into the vestibule. I was put in charge of decorating this year, and I think my parents probably regret that decision. There are very few surfaces in the lobby that aren't covered with some sort of Christmas decoration, and I am not ashamed.

"Nope! Get out!" someone yells from the front desk.

"I just want to—"

"Nope! Out! You are on vacation. Get out!"

"John, I—"

"Delaney, I love you for coming to check on us, but you trained me on everything that has to be done for this dinner. Now go. Out! Go home. I don't want to see you again until after New Year's."

John walks around the counter, takes me by the arm, and walks me right back out the front door.

I stand on the porch for a minute or two in silence. I know that I'm on vacation, but it would have been nice to spend some time with the people that I work with. Guess that's not going to happen.

Alrighty then . . . I guess I'm going home after all.

Chapter 2

Delaney

I can just see the street from where I'm sitting, and I can tell it's shaping up to be a lovely night. Cold, but lovely. I turn my focus to the inside of the restaurant, and I'm pretty much instantly in love with everything around me. Christmas lights, garland, and a big, beautiful Christmas tree full of decorations. To be honest, I shouldn't be taking in all the sights around me; I should be paying attention to my date. But instead of enjoying myself on this Friday night blind date, I'm wishing I wasn't here. I'd rather be anywhere else than here. Hell, I think I'd rather be at the dentist than here. Why, you might ask? The answer is simple.

I am bored out of my mind!

I'm sitting here listening to the idiot across from me go on and on about his line of work. First, he babbled about some dumb game he likes to play. He told me about the characters, scenes, and levels, and how long it took him to defeat each level. And now he's yapping about what he does for a living. He hasn't even given me a chance to say anything about myself.

I already know what you do, ass!

This has to be the most boring date I've ever had to endure. But that's what I get when I agree to a blind date. This shmuck is Joy's husband's work colleague turned bromance. According to Joy, the two of them had gotten to be best friends over the last five months. How they are buddies, I'll never know. But it's becoming completely clear to me that even though Joy and I have been best friends for eight years, she still has absolutely no idea what I look for in a man. Hell, *I'm* not even sure anymore. But what I do know is that this idiot isn't it.

"I'll be right back," my idiot date says as he stands and rushes from the table toward the restroom.

Thank god.

Maybe he'll flush himself and save me the trouble of having to listen to him anymore. I roll my eyes and shake my head as I grab my phone from my purse.

I need to ask you something, Joy. What the HELL were you thinking when you set me up with this idiot? Good lord!

I set my phone on the table and put my head in my hands. I've only been sitting there for a few seconds when a familiar, deep voice causes me to look up.

Oh, my god . . . It's the man from yesterday!

"Not having a good time, huh?"

He's even more handsome tonight than he was last night. How is that even possible?

"Is it that transparent?" I ask with a smile.

The man smiles back at me. My goodness is he freaking yummy.

"Just a little bit. I'm Flynn," he says as he reaches his hand out.

I used to know a Flynn back when Dylan and I were kids. I had the biggest crush on him, but it was crazy because he was my brother's best friend. I'm pretty sure there is some unwritten rule somewhere that warns against dating your sibling's friend, so I kept my crush to myself.

I reach my hand out to shake his, and three things occur as our skin touches. First, I am hit with an extremely strong déjà vu moment. Like I've already met this man before. Second, I feel as if sparks shoot from my hand to his and back again. And third, heat begins to flood to my cheeks, and I instantly know that I'm probably blushing like crazy again.

How is it possible that a complete stranger has me clenching my thighs together?

"I'm Delaney. It's nice to meet you, Flynn," I say with a smile.

He continues to hold my hand, then brings it up to his lips and places a gentle kiss on the top of my hand. His eyes never leave mine and I am suddenly very aware of the fact that I'm turned on by how much of a gentleman Flynn is.

"The pleasure is all mine, beautiful," he says smoothly.

Good. Freaking. Lord.

He releases my hand, which is when I remember I'm currently on a date, so I look toward the restrooms to see if the idiot is coming back yet. He is nowhere to be seen, so I look back at Flynn.

"I know this is a little unorthodox, but I was wondering if I could possibly get your number?"

Yes! Take my number. Hell, take me!

I still feel very flustered, so I clear my throat and take a deep breath to try to calm myself. "Very forward of you, don't you think?"

Flynn stares at me. "Yes. But I almost always get what I want," he says smoothly.

I smile as my face and my body heat up even more. "Hmm, this might be one of those times when you *don't* get what you want. I am on a date right now, ya know," I say with sass, then roll my eyes.

He smiles back at me, but then narrows his eyes. "Right. You mean with the douchebag who left you sitting here so he could go bang the waitress in the bathroom?"

"Are you for fu— I mean, are you for real?"

Anyone who knows me knows I have quite an attitude, a temper, and a foul mouth. Few swear words are off limits to me, and I've found over the years that not many can handle how outspoken I always am. Which is probably why I'm still single. I really don't want to scare this Flynn away before I have the chance to know more about him, so I want to try to keep profanities to an absolute minimum. For now.

"Yep," he replies with a pop. "I was washing my hands when they flew into the bathroom and locked themselves in a stall."

"What a fucking asshole," I say so fast I don't even have time to censor myself.

Well, there goes that whole no profanities thing.

Flynn lets out a deep laugh, then bends down so he's super close to me. "You want to get out of here with me, Delaney?" he asks with a wink as he offers me his hand.

I've never done anything like this before, but there definitely is something familiar about Flynn. I can't freaking place it, but I know it has to be something. I look at him for a moment while I consider what I want to say. Joy did tell me that I should live my life and I think that's what I need to do.

Carpe diem.

"I really do," I say with a smile.

I toss my phone into my purse and take Flynn's hand. He helps me to stand, and I quickly realize he definitely has to be more than six foot. I'm five-foot-seven and I'm wearing two-inch heels, and he still towers over me.

My goodness, this man really is a god.

I feel a familiar blush creep up my cheeks and a warmth spreads south. It feels as if massive butterflies are flying around in my stomach, and I have to grab the table to steady myself. Flynn smiles and winks as if he knows the affect he has on me. He helps me into my jacket, then quickly pulls his jacket on, which he had hanging on his arm, then he wraps his arm around my shoulder.

What the hell? You only live once.

I wrap my arm around his waist as we head toward the door. He stops by one of the waiters who's standing not far from the door.

"My bill is paid, but hers isn't. Her ex-date will take care of it. He's in the bathroom banging one of your waitresses at the moment though, so it may be a few minutes," he says before we start to walk.

The look on the waiter's face is absolutely hilarious, and we leave the restaurant in fits of laughter.

This man . . .

He's definitely got balls—and talk about a contact high. The minute Flynn put his arm around me, I felt insane heat coming off him. That warm, fuzzy feeling should have ceased to exist the moment we stepped outside. It's winter . . . in Upstate New York. It's so much more than cold; it's frigid and snowy, and I should be freezing. But at this very moment? All I feel is the heat coming off Flynn and the heat that is quickly spreading throughout me.

Flynn stops walking, then steps in front of me. Looking down at me, he smiles as he tucks a strand of hair behind my ear. "Do you want to go back to my hotel with me?" he asks in that deep, sexy voice of his.

Hotel.

Which means he isn't from here. And it also means he'll most likely be leaving at some point. A small ping of disappointment hits me, but I do my best to brush it off as quickly as it appeared.

"Yes, I do. But . . . " I trail off, suddenly feeling ridiculously shy.

He smiles, then presses a small kiss to my forehead, which totally takes me by surprise.

"But you just met me, you don't know me, and you're nervous. I totally get it," he says calmly, like I hadn't just led him to believe I was going home with him.

If possible, Flynn takes a step closer to me, and my entire body shudders, but not from the cold. I've never been this affected by a man in my entire life. Something about him feels so freaking familiar, but I still can't figure out what it is. My body feels like it's on fire, and all I can think about is going to his hotel and getting out of this dress. But reason starts to seep in, which forces the wild woman within to calm the hell down.

"I'm sorry," I say nervously. "I know I left with you, and you didn't force me to, I really wanted to . . . but I've never done this before. And yes, I'm nervous. Very nervous."

Flynn smiles down at me and pulls me against his strong chest, then wraps his arms around me. I instantly melt into him and wrap my arms around his waist. Why this feels so natural and right is beyond me. I feel like we have history and we've known each other for years, which is crazy because I just met this man not even a half hour ago. Flynn clears his throat, which pulls me back to the moment. I release him and pull back to look up at him.

"I'm not ready for this night to be over yet, Delaney. How about we grab some coffee, and we can get to know one another better?"

I look at him for a moment while I consider what I want to say. I want to go back to his place so badly, but I know I wouldn't feel comfortable with that. Him offering me an alternative is amazing. I love coffee, so a coffee date sounds perfect. I really want to say yes, but I legit cannot wait to go home and take off this stupid dress and these stupid heels that Joy picked out for me.

I think about it for a few more seconds, then decide to say screw it and be ballsy for once in my life. I'm going to suggest something I wouldn't normally suggest.

"Yes, Flynn. I would love to get coffee with you. But I'll tell you what," I say, before I pause for a moment. "Why don't you come back to my place, and I'll make us coffee and we can talk and hang out. Maybe watch a movie or something?"

Flynn stares at me with his beautiful, rich brown eyes and then does something I was not expecting. He leans down and crashes his lips to mine. This isn't a sweet, sensual kiss; this is a hard, claiming kiss. A kiss to end all other kisses. This kiss means business. What that business is, I don't know, but I am damn sure I'm going to find out.

As soon as possible, I hope.

We stand there on the sidewalk and make out like a couple of teenagers for a few minutes, and I'm completely breathless when we finally pull apart.

"I'd love to come back to your place," he says with a shit-eating grin on his face. "But only if you're sure. I don't want to make you uncomfortable. You could tell me you want to part ways for now, and I will completely respect that. It's your call."

"I'm sure. I'll be honest with you, Flynn. I feel like I know you . . . which, I know, is crazy."

Flynn's posture visibly changes, and I can't help but wonder why. Maybe he feels it too? He steps beside me and takes my hand, giving it a gentle squeeze.

"We can talk more once we get where we're going. Where to, my Delaney?" he asks as if I've been his for years.

The thought gives me major butterflies and I can't help but feel warm all over. I think I'm going to be in trouble with this one.

Chapter 3

Delaney

O ne of the only things I can think as we start walking down the sidewalk again is that I've only known this man for a few minutes, but he is already working his way into my heart. Well, actually it kind of seems like he is already *in* my heart. It just feels so natural to be walking hand in hand with Flynn.

We walk the three-minute walk to my house in silence, still holding hands like we've been with each other for years. As we reach my front sidewalk, I pull my hand from Flynn's, then walk a few steps ahead of him up onto my porch. I take my key out of my purse, then slip it into the lock.

"So . . . how old are you? Where did you go to school? Are you from around here?"

I don't mean to blurt out all the questions at once, but everything seems to come out in one breath. I close my eyes and take a deep breath as I turn my key in the lock. A few seconds later, I can feel Flynn's presence directly behind me, and I know he didn't wait on the sidewalk. His hand slips to my right side, and I can feel his breath near my ear.

"I'm thirty, and I grew up not far from here," he replies. "How about you?"

I slowly turn to face Flynn, and I'm suddenly very aware of how small my front porch actually is. We're so close that he must be able to feel my heart pounding. For a moment, my voice seems to get lost, and I can't reply. The intensity of this moment has me utterly flabbergasted. I clear my throat, then finally find my voice.

"Uh . . . sorry. I just turned thirty-one, and I was born and raised here."

He smiles at me. "Ah. Very nice," he replies as he slips one hand onto the doorknob behind me.

Being pressed up against Flynn has me forgetting that I unlocked the door and that we're still standing here in the freezing cold night.

Good lord, take me right here, right now.

"Shall we?" he asks, waiting for me to give the final word.

"Yes," I respond, just barely above a whisper.

Flynn turns the knob, then pushes the door open with a little more force than necessary, and the door bangs against the wall.

"Oops, sorry about that," Flynn says as he scoops me up into his arms, causing me to squeal.

"Oh my god, Flynn! Put me down before you hurt yourself!"

I'm not a skinny girl by any stretch of the imagination, so the fact that he lifts me as if I don't weigh much surprises the hell out of me. He carries me over the threshold and into my house, then sets me down as soon as we are inside. His lips are on mine in an instant, and he kicks the door shut. Again, harder than necessary, but who gives a fuck? He quickly spins me, pressing me up against the wall next to the door, but then he pulls away.

"What is it?" I ask breathlessly.

He shakes his head, then opens the door and retrieves my keys from the lock, then shuts the door again and locks it. Then he turns and hands me my keys.

"Nothing. Just can't be too careful," he replies.

We quickly kick off our shoes, then take our coats off and hang them on the coatrack. As soon as the coats are hung, he throws his arm around me and pulls me to his chest. My hands land on his rock-hard chest and I take a breath and close my eyes.

I am not going to sleep with Flynn. I am not going to sleep with Flynn.

I slowly open my eyes and find his scorching gaze. He leans down and gently places his lips against mine. This kiss is gentle and sweet, nothing like the last two we shared. He pulls back, then steps aside.

"So . . . I was told there would be coffee," he says with a smile.

"Yes. Yes, you were," I reply as I walk past him.

I toss my purse and keys onto the small table across from my door, then flick on a light switch in the living room. My entire living room comes to life. Christmas lights and garland hang on pretty much every available surface. My nine-foot Christmas tree is decorated with four massive strands of colored lights, at least a hundred different ornaments, and a large, lighted star.

"Holy fuck," Flynn whispers under his breath, and I can't help but let out a giggle.

Christmas has always been my absolute favorite holiday, and I'm not afraid to say it, or show it.

"Yes. I know. I'm Christmas crazy," I say proudly.

"I know," Flynn replies, but then he sucks in a sharp breath.

"What do you mean, you know?" I ask, suddenly semi-alarmed.

Flynn looks like a deer in headlights for only a second before the look disappears.

"I mean, I can tell by this room. There doesn't seem to be a surface in this room that doesn't have something Christmas-y on it. It's beautiful."

The unsure moment passes quickly, and my sudden alarm disappears. I stare at Flynn while he stares at my Christmas tree. I move across the living room and stop near my massive sectional to grab the remote. I turn on the TV, then toss the remote back onto the couch.

"Please make yourself at home," I say as I motion toward the couch. "I'm going to get changed real fast, then I'll get the coffee started."

Flynn walks past my fireplace and is heading toward the couch when he suddenly stops right in front of the fireplace. It only takes me a quick second to realize what he's looking at. My mantle is lined with pictures. I have some of me, my brother, and our parents, some of me with my friends, and one very special picture of me, my brother, and his best friend, Flynn. I walk up next to him and see he's holding the picture of Dylan, Flynn, and I.

"That's me, my twin brother Dylan, and his best friend, Flynn. We were thirteen." I reply, as if he had asked the question. "We took that picture the day Flynn and his parents moved away. Dylan was miserable for weeks."

"Ah."

"Yeah, it was a rough time for us all. Dylan and Flynn were inseparable since we all started kindergarten. After Flynn left, my brother really shut down and kept to himself a lot. Even though my parents kept in touch with Flynn's parents, I don't think Dylan and Flynn kept in touch much after he left."

I look back at Flynn to see he's just staring at me. He has a weird look on his face—almost sad, or emotional. He notices that I'm looking at him again, so he quickly changes his expression. It happens so fast that I'm not even sure if I really saw the emotion or if I was imagining it. I offer a small smile, then continue.

"I'm sorry. I know you didn't ask but I saw you looking at that picture and thought I'd explain who it was."

He puts the picture down and turns to me. "All good. I like seeing pictures of you. You were a cutie. Anyway, you go get changed. I'm going to see if I can find a movie for us to watch."

"Deal." I smile, then turn and head down the hall. "But no macho-guy crap!" I call out as I reach my bedroom door.

I hear him chuckle, then call out, "Fine, but that also means no chick flicks!"

"Smartass!" I call back as I open my door.

I lean against my closed door and take a few breaths. I'm not sure what just happened, but it was something. Flynn almost looked pained when I was talking about my brother and his best friend. The only thing I can think of is that he had had a similar experience or something. My heart clenches and tears come to my eyes as I think about Flynn. I had such a thing for him, and it hurt when he moved away. For a while, I swore he might have felt something for me too, but it turns out I was just his 'best friend's little sister.' His words.

I quickly blink away the tears that threaten to fall, then take a deep breath and open my eyes.

"Come on, Delaney, no sense in living in the past when you have a gorgeous man in your living room," I whisper to myself, then step away from the door.

I quickly take off the stupid dress Joy had picked out for my date and toss it into my laundry basket. I pull open my dresser and grab a pair of black yoga pants and a UCONN t-shirt before I throw my hair up into a messy bun. I open my door and head out to the kitchen, where I quickly start a pot of coffee. I walk over to the couch, but don't sit.

"I have some of my brother's clothes in my spare bedroom if you want to change into something more comfortable?"

"Trying to get me naked already, huh?"

My eyes go wide, and I know my cheeks instantly go red, which of course makes Flynn burst into a fit of laugher.

"No! I just . . . I thought sweatpants and a t-shirt would be more comfortable than dress clothes!" I blurt out as I cover my face with my hands.

Flynn reaches up and pulls me onto his lap, then takes my hands and pulls them from my face, still laughing.

"I was totally messing with you, Delaney. Do you think you'll have something that'll fit me? I am super freaking tall, after all," he replies, and I giggle.

"My brother is a little shorter than you, but they should be fine. Come on."

I stand and lead him toward my spare bedroom which is down the hall.

Chapter 4

Delaney

I push open the door and flick on the light. The room I walk into doesn't look anything like the rest of my house. Where the rest of my house is nice, clean, and decorated to the max, this room is a plain, blah-looking mess. I never did much to this room because it was always just me living here, and when Dylan moved to Italy, I told him he could leave the stuff he didn't want to take with him here. The whole room literally looks like I just moved in. There are boxes everywhere, and the bed is just a box spring and mattress on the floor with a nightstand on either side. The dresser still has blankets tied around it from the movers, and in the corner is a leather recliner and some more boxes.

"Dylan left a bunch of shit here when his job offered him a position in their Italy office a few months ago. A lot of workout clothes, hoodies, and stuff. I stole some hoodies, but there are a bunch left, along with T-shirts and sweatpants. They're in that box over by the closet door." I point across the room.

"Thanks. So, your brother moved to Italy?"

"Yes. He's going to be there for the next four months, then he'll come home for a month before he goes back to Italy."

"Wow. That's incredible. What does he do?"

"He works for a PR firm," I reply. "Anyway, feel free to pick whatever you'd be comfortable in."

"Thanks."

"No problem. I'll give you some privacy."

If I'm being completely honest, I don't want to give Flynn privacy. I want nothing more than to throw my arms around his neck and kiss the fuck out of him again. I also really want to find out exactly what he can do. In the bedroom, of course. But I feel like thinking about sexual stuff is crazy. I literally just met this man, and I'm already thinking about what it would be like to have sex with him. There has to be something wrong with me.

I glance up at Flynn and the look on his face tells me I'm not the only one thinking about what it would be like. Suddenly overcome with this extreme feeling of pure lust, I realize that I have to get out of here. I turn and start to move out the doorway to head back into the living room, but Flynn catches my wrist and stops me. He pulls me to his chest and wraps his arms around me. As if it's the most natural thing in the world, my arms go up around his neck and we hold each other close.

"Flynn, I have to tell you . . . I know we just met last night, but it feels like I already know you. Like, *know you*, know you. Not just met you. Is that crazy?" I ask, looking up into his eyes.

He looks at me as if he's trying to figure out how to respond, and his lack of an answer makes me nervous. Maybe I said too much. I drop my arms and try to back up. "I'm sorry, I didn't mean to weird you out or anything."

Flynn's grip on my waist tightens and he pulls me to his chest again. "You definitely didn't weird me out, Delaney. I don't think you could ever weird me out," he replies, then stops.

He smiles down at me for a moment, but then his look turns more serious. He lets out a breath, and it's almost as if he hadn't been breathing since he pulled me against his chest. He leans down and places a small kiss on my forehead. "And no, it's not crazy. I happen to agree. It feels like I've known you forever, like you're meant to be mine. To be my girl."

Oh my goodness.

For a moment I'm totally floored. I'm not sure what to do or say. The intensity of his gaze is almost too much to handle, and I want to look away. But at the same time, I couldn't force myself to look away even if I wanted to.

"I don't—" I close my eyes, take a deep breath, and hold it for a few seconds before I blow it out. I open my eyes again and smile. "To be completely honest, I don't even know what to say to that, Flynn. I don't think I've ever felt such a connection to anyone before in my life."

"How about we take it day by day, and we get to know each other and see what happens?"

"I would love that," I answer honestly.

"Okay good, because so would I. Come on, let's go back to the living room. I can't be this close to a bed and not think about getting you in it."

I feel my cheeks heat as we turn to leave my spare room. "Wait . . . don't you want to change?"

"Nah, it's okay. I'm actually thinking maybe I should head back to my hotel now instead."

A ping of disappointment hits me, and I quickly look down to try to hide it, but apparently it's written all over my face. Flynn places a finger under my chin and lifts it so I meet his gaze.

"Even though I know you just started the coffee, and I would love to stay, I should leave now. Because if I don't, I'm going to end up taking you to bed, and I don't want to do that just yet. I meant what I said. I want to take it day by day and really get to know you. And I want you to really get to know me. Okay?"

Between what he just said and the fact that I am staring deeply into his eyes, I am completely flustered. I feel like my face is probably bright-ass red again for the millionth time since I met Flynn. I lightly bite my lower lip, and Flynn lets out a low growl—an actual fucking growl—which shocks the hell out of me.

"Please don't do that, Delaney." He leans down and takes me by surprise once again with another claiming kiss that is full of heat and passion.

Every kiss seems hotter than the last and I'm struggling to keep myself from jumping Flynn's bones right here and right now. By the time he pulls back, I'm totally breathless again.

Goodness, this man can kiss! I bet he's amazing in the bedroom . . .

I shake my head to try to get that thought out there as soon as possible.

"Damn!" I exclaim, and Flynn laughs.

"Come on," he says, then takes my hand and leads me to the door.

As we pass by the table where my purse is, I reach in and grab my phone.

"Hey, Flynn?"

He stops and turns to me. "Yes?"

"I know we just met, but I was wondering if I could possibly get your phone number?" I smile, then bite my lower lip again.

Flynn lets out a deep laugh. "Yes. You can definitely have my number," he replies as he leans down and gently kisses me on the forehead.

A few moments later, we exchange numbers, then Flynn slips on his shoes and grabs his coat off the hook. Once he's all bundled up, he turns to me and pulls me into another hug. He places a gentle kiss on my forehead, says goodnight, then walks out onto the front stoop and pulls the door closed behind him. I walk over and lock both locks just as my phone vibrates in my hand.

Thank you for an amazing night, my Delaney.

His Delaney. Drool.

A huge smile hits my face as I quickly type out a reply.

No, thank you. And thank you for rescuing me from that sucky-ass date.

I'm glad I was there to rescue you.

Swoon.

It dawns on me that I never even asked Flynn if he was single, and I feel really stupid. He could have a girlfriend or wife back wherever he is from.

I'm so sorry. I never even asked . . . I hope I didn't take you away from anyone.

Nope. I was having dinner alone.

Not exactly the answer I was hoping for. I was hoping he would expand his answer a little. I have no idea how to ask Flynn if he's single without just coming out and asking, so I guess that's what I'm going to have to do.

Are you single, Flynn?

Little text bubbles appear, then disappear, then reappear and disappear once again. I can't help but feel a little nervous. I'm not sure why his answer is taking so long. Maybe he isn't single. Maybe I made a huge mistake asking him to come over. And kissing him . . . Oh geez. This could be bad. I stare at my phone and wait, and my heart skips a beat when it finally chimes again.

Delaney, yes! Of course I'm single. Do you really think I would have approached you if I wasn't?

I don't know. I mean, I would hope you wouldn't, but to be honest, I don't know anything about you. Just your name.

I'm really hoping I don't scare him off with my untrusting ways, but I kind of can't help it. If life has taught me anything, it's that you never know what's going to happen.

I get it. Yes, I am very single. And I can't wait for you to get to know more about me.

I can't wait, either.

Anyway, have a good night, Delaney.

You too. Talk to you soon.

Yes, you will.

I can't help but think I'm in trouble when it comes to Flynn. I already want to talk to him as much as possible and learn as much as I can as quickly as I can. There is just something about him, a familiarity, and I don't think it's just me that feels it. He seemed to be just as affected as I was. It also seemed like he wanted to say more, but it was like something was holding him back.

I go back into the kitchen and switch off the coffeepot, then walk over to the couch and grab the remote and turn the TV off. Then I turn off all the lights in the living room, but leave the Christmas tree lit up.

So beautiful.

I stand there for a few minutes and admire the beauty I created this year. I usually go for white lights, but this year I decided to go crazy with multicolored lights, and I'm really liking how everything came out. I would sit here in the dark and admire my Christmas lights all night if I could, but I'm meeting Joy for another coffee date tomorrow and staying up all night would be nuts.

I walk up to my Christmas tree and turn off the power strip, then walk down the hall to my bedroom.

Chapter 5

Flynn

It takes every ounce of strength I have in me to walk out of Delaney's house. I wanted nothing more than to throw her on the bed and make her mine. Right then and there. But I know that can't happen yet. A lot of things have to happen before we get anywhere close to getting into bed together—and those things are going to be tough as fuck. So tough that it's entirely possible that she'll walk away from me. She might never want to see me again. It'll suck and it'll likely hurt like hell, but it would be her right. I opened this doorway when I approached her and didn't tell her who I was. I gave her my first name, but I didn't give her my last name. And that's because it's a last name she would have recognized instantly, and I wasn't ready for her to dismiss me yet.

I knew it was going to be difficult to see her and not tell her who I was, but I had been prepared for difficult. What I wasn't prepared for was for today to be downright torture. Sitting there watching her on that pitiful date, and then seeing her date and the waitress fly into that bathroom stall, was horrible. I wanted to fucking kill the asshole, but I used that as my opportunity to approach Delaney.

I knew she would either recognize me instantly or she wouldn't at all. It had been years since we'd seen each other, and I didn't exactly look the same as I did the last time we saw each other. Where my hair used to be light brown, it is now very dark, almost black. I've grown to be almost six-foot-three, and I have bulked up—I'm not scrawny like I used to be. Plus, I have tattoos up and down one of my arms. The only thing that is the same is my chocolate brown eyes. I was banking on her not recognizing me, and that's exactly what happened.

Regardless of which reaction I got, however, I was ready to handle either reaction. As long as I finally got to see her and talk to her again. What I wasn't ready for was all the feelings I had for her back then come rushing back in an instant. Despite how I felt then, I know she didn't share in the feelings, and it sucked. To her, I was just her twin brother's best friend. And sure, that's what I was, but then my family moved, and everything changed. I never forgot about Delaney. Hell, I even looked her up online a bunch of times just so I could see pictures of her. I wanted more than anything to come back into her life and tell her how I felt and how I still feel, but I figured she would just dismiss me because Dylan and I had been best friends. I've actually been ready to act on my feelings for a while but work always kept me super busy and I never had a chance to come back here. But things changed and I'm ready now. More than ready, actually. Of course, in order to do that, I have to tell Delaney who I really am, sooner rather than later. I'm not sure how she is going to take it. I'm hoping she gives me a chance, but I'm not sure. One thing I am sure about is that everything is going to change the moment she finds out who I am, and I'm not quite ready for that just yet.

I realize that I'm absolutely being a coward, but I can't help it. I've been in love with this woman since before I really knew what love was. Talking to her again proved one major thing: Despite the amount of time that's gone by, I'm still in love with her and want her, and I won't stop until she is mine.

I pull the zipper of my jacket the rest of the way up and make my way back to my hotel room. Thankfully it isn't far from her house because it is ridiculously cold tonight. Any longer of a walk and I would probably freeze to death on the side of the road. Okay, that's being a bit dramatic, even for me, but it really is freaking cold tonight. I certainly haven't missed the frigid cold temps of winter in Upstate New York or all the snow, but I would definitely deal with it again if it meant being with Delaney. She is everything I want in a partner, and dealing with winter in Upstate New York would be a breeze if it meant I would get to spend my life with her.

A few minutes later, I come around the corner and approach my hotel, which is situated across the street from the lake. I step up onto the porch, then turn to look at the town. There might be a lot of snow on the ground, but it paints a pretty picture. I could definitely live here again and raise a family. I lived here in North Shore until I was a teenager, but then my family moved away. I came back to visit once I was older, but it has been years since that visit. I wasn't ready to stay then, but I am now. A chill runs through me as I turn back around and walk into the hotel.

"Welcome back," the concierge says as I approach the front desk. "Did you enjoy the restaurant?"

"Yes, I did. Thank you for the recommendation," I reply as I walk toward the elevators.

"Of course, sir. Have a great night."

"You, too," I call out as I continue toward the elevator.

Once inside, I hit my floor number, then lean back against the wall and close my eyes. I didn't mean to be rude to the concierge, but tonight's events were a lot to take in. I want nothing more than to go up to my room, have a big-ass drink, and pass the hell out. I open my eyes just in time to hear the elevator ding, signaling I've reached my floor. The doors slide open, so I step out and make my way to my room. I pull my room card from my pocket and slip it into the door. Once the green light appears, I open the door and step inside. I'm walking across the room when my phone chimes, so I remove it from my pocket and set it on the bed. I pull off my coat and scarf, then remove my shoes before I sit on the edge of the bed and grab my phone. I'm surprised to see Delaney's name pop up on the screen, but I'd be lying if I said I wasn't a bit excited, too.

I just wanted to say, it really was nice meeting you tonight.
Oh babe, you have no idea . . .
It was great to meet you as well.
I know we already said our goodnights, but what are you up to?
Thinking about you and how badly I fucked up by not coming clean right off the bat.
You can text me any time. Doesn't matter when. And I just got back to my hotel. About to have a drink. Hbu?

Text bubbles appear almost immediately, and I don't move from where I am.

Maybe I should have a drink too. My mind is all over the place tonight. I'm thinking about you and how I really feel like we've met before. You seem so familiar to me.
This is totally going to blow up in my face.
A drink couldn't hurt. Might help to calm the nerves a bit. And I feel the same way.
Is it crazy to say that I can't wait to see you again?
Not crazy at all.
No, it's not crazy. I feel the same way. You should have that drink and then try to get some sleep.
I want to talk more.
I'd love nothing more, but I can't do this tonight.
We'll talk more. I promise.
Okay. Well . . . good night, Flynn.
Goodnight, Delaney.

I place my phone on the bed, then start pulling my clothes off. I'm completely exhausted and feel like I could collapse, but I need a shower. Once I'm in my boxers, I stomp my way into the bathroom and turn the shower on. I knew this was going to be a very trying few days, but I didn't think just being around Delaney would be so completely exhausting. I don't know how long I'm going to be able to hold out before I tell her the truth. It's not fair to her, or me, but mostly to her. She deserves to know the truth. Regardless of what happens, she needs to know.

To be completely honest, I never should have kept my last name a secret to begin with. I should have just come clean right off the bat, but I was seriously worried she would just dismiss me. I wanted her to get to know me first. Get to know me as a single, adult man. Not a teenage boy that was her brother's best friend. If I could redo the night, I would have just told her my last name and gone from there. But it's too late. Now all I can do is hope she gives me a chance to explain myself.

Chapter 6

Delaney

"Joy! How could you set me up with that moron?" I ask my best friend the next day.

"I'm sorry! I thought you guys would hit it off. He seemed really nice when I met him at Jason's company dinner back in July."

"Not only did we *not* hit it off, but he left the table to go bang the waitress in the bathroom," I say, then burst out laughing at the face Joy gives me.

"Are you kidding me?!"

"I wish I was."

Joy's face looks like a sad little deer that just watched its mother get shot. I was semi-mad at her for even thinking the two of us would click, but I definitely can't continue to let her think I'm even remotely upset about what happened.

"But for real, I don't care. I'm glad he left the table because I literally got swept off my feet by the six-foot-something guy we saw at the coffee shop."

"How could you not lead with that?! Tell me everything!" Joy says as she sips her coffee.

I tell Joy everything that happened last night. She is my best friend, so I leave no small detail out. She gives many different faces while I go through the events of the night, but the face that she gives me when I tell her that I invited Flynn over to my place had to be the best face ever. Joy knows me better than anyone, and she knows that doing something like that was so out of character for me, but I can tell by the smile on her face she's pleased that I did it.

We continue gossiping, drinking more coffee than we should, and finally, an hour later, we're ready to head out. Joy and I meet at this coffee shop sometimes four times a week for our bestie coffee catch-up, so it's no surprise to me when the guy behind the counter calls us by our names and says he'll see us in a day or two as we walk out the door.

"Girl, I can't even believe you met this dude while being ditched by Bryant. But it is so his loss!"

"Ah. That's his name!" I giggle. "I kept calling him the idiot."

We both burst into laughter as my phone chimes in my back pocket.

"Ooh, who is that?" Joy teases as we walk toward her car.

I smack her arm, then grab my phone out of my pocket.

"It's a text from my brother. Oh my god, he's coming home next week for a few meetings. Wants to know if I want to meet up for dinner!" I squeal with excitement.

"That's awesome, Del!" Joy says as we reach her car. "I have to head to work, but I'll call you later."

"Sounds good. Love ya, bestie," I say as she climbs into her car and drives away.

I take off down the street and head toward my house. The good thing about living so close to downtown is that I can walk everywhere if need be. I do have an all-wheel drive SUV, but today I chose to bundle up and walk to the coffee shop. Friends from out of town always say that I have serious problems because I can deal with the temperatures and snow amounts, but this has always been my home and I can't imagine living anywhere else.

I'm pretty much frozen by the time I reach my front stoop, but the walk felt good. I get myself inside and start to take all my layers off, then walk down the hall and into my bedroom. It's only a little after eleven in the morning, but I already feel like I need a nap. I was up for a while after Flynn left last night. I couldn't shake the feeling that I've met him before, plus I couldn't believe how well we clicked. I even had a drink like he suggested, and I still couldn't sleep. If I didn't have my coffee date with Joy, I probably would have stayed in bed all day.

I put my phone on my nightstand, then take off my jeans and sweat-shirt. I grab my sleep shorts and slide them on, then pull back my covers and climb into bed. I almost always sleep in shorts and a tank top. I hate feeling suffocated or trapped by pants or long sleeves when I sleep. It might be winter, but my house has an amazing heating system. I currently have three comforters on my bed—two of which are big, fluffy down comforters—so I definitely don't get cold. I snuggle into my fluff of blankets and close my eyes. I start thinking about Flynn again, and that's the last thing I remember.

The next thing I know, my phone is chiming away on my nightstand. I pick it up and notice the time. It's a little after five, which means I slept for six hours.

That was some nap.

The first thing I see is a text from Flynn, followed by two from Dylan. I figure my brother can wait—especially with the time difference—so I open Flynn's message first.

Hey, gorgeous, what are you up to today?

A big smile comes to my face, and I nibble my bottom lip. This man is already making me feel things I've never felt for any of my ex-boyfriends. That should scare me, but it doesn't. If anything, it intrigues me.

Hey! Not much. Just woke up from a bit of a long nap, actually. I had coffee this morning with my bestie, but I was so tired that I passed out as soon as I got home. What are you doing?

I send the message and close his text thread, then open my brother's.

Hey, sis! Did you get my voicemail? I'm coming to town on Wednesday for a few work meetings. I was hoping we could have

lunch on Wednesday, and then Christmas Eve dinner at the B&B on Friday night?

I'm so glad my brother and I have stayed close even though he lives in Italy now. I don't know what I would do without him.

Hey, Dylan!! Yes! Both sound awesome. I can't wait to see you! Sounds good! See you on Wednesday. Ciao!

I drop my phone next to me and roll onto my side, pulling my blankets further up. I should really get up, but I don't want to right now. My phone chimes again and I'm quick to pick it up. It's Flynn.

Sounds like fun. Just wanted to see what you were up to. Thought I would ask if maybe you'd like some company? I thought we could watch that movie.

Tempting. Very tempting indeed.

Hmm . . . I do enjoy movie nights. Pizza and a movie would really seal the deal.

I probably shouldn't have said 'seal the deal' because it makes it sound sexual, but it's too late to take the text back now.

I could go for pizza and a movie.

What the hell?

Okay, let's do it!

I throw my blankets back and jump up out of bed as soon as I send the message. I quickly make the bed, then walk into my en suite bathroom and grab my brush. I pull it through my wavy blonde hair a few times, then pull my hair up into a high, flirty ponytail. I pull a few strands of hair free here and there, then check my makeup. Not bad considering I just woke up from a six-hour nap. Next, I walk back into my room and pull out my favorite Italy zip-up hoodie and slip it on over my tank top, then change into my favorite black yoga pants that make my ass look fantastic. My phone chimes a few seconds later and I grab it all too quickly.

Awesome. What time are you thinking?

Is now too soon?

I just got up and got freshened up, so whenever is good for you is good for me.

Okay, good. Can you come open the door then ;-)

Oh my god! He's already here!

I close my eyes and take a few deep breaths. "Okay. It's okay. I can do this," I say to myself as I turn and head toward the front door.

I take another deep breath before I pull the door open.

"Hey there," I say with a huge smile.

"Hey, gorgeous," Flynn replies as he walks into the house.

Once he's inside, I close and lock the door. I turn just as Flynn shrugs his coat off and hangs it on the coatrack. He looks even better today than he did last night. He's wearing a tight shirt underneath a gray zip-up hoodie that's hanging open, sweatpants, and sneakers, which he kicks off near the door. I smile at the gesture. I go to walk past Flynn to lead him toward the couch, but he leans in and wraps his arms around me, pulling me into a hug. I'm slightly tense at first because he kind of catches me off guard, but I quickly melt into him and lean up to wrap my arms around his neck.

"It feels good to hold you," Flynn whispers in my ear, giving me goosebumps. "I hope you know how hard it was to leave last night."

I let out a small giggle. "Believe me, I know what you mean. Come on—you find us a movie to watch, and I'll order us pizza. And last night's rules still apply. No macho-guy crap and no chick flicks," I say with a giggle as I walk into the kitchen.

"Deal," Flynn says as he releases me, then walks over and picks a spot on my sectional to get comfy.

I quickly order a pizza, then open the fridge. "Would you like a drink?"

"Yes, please. Do you have any beer?"

"I don't, but I have soda, water, wine, and whiskey."

"Hmm . . . Wine is fine. Thank you."

I pour two glasses of wine, then cork the bottle and leave it on the counter. I pick up both glasses and walk to the couch to hand Flynn a glass. I plop down on the sectional, but I don't sit right next to him, leaving a cushion empty between us.

Flynn smiles. "I don't stink, you know."

"What? No . . . I know! I just . . . I wasn't sure if you wanted a little space or anything."

Nope. That wasn't awkward at all.

Flynn chuckles and I know he was only teasing me.

"So, what are we watching?" I ask, taking a sip of my wine.

I don't want to drink it too fast. I might be Italian, but I can't hold my liquor for anything.

"Well, we agreed to no macho-guy crap or chick flicks, so I picked horror/paranormal." He smiles at me.

My eyes go wide, and I look away.

Crap.

That totally backfired on me. I'm one hundred percent a major chicken-shit. I bring my gaze back to him and he looks more amused than before.

"What's wrong?" he asks with a cheeky smile on his gorgeous face.

He's totally fucking with me. He knows it, and now I know it. But I'm game. I'll play.

"Will you protect me?" I ask innocently.

"Of course I will. Come here," he says, motioning for me to move closer.

I stand and grab my fuzzy blanket off the other end of the sectional, then join Flynn. I sit and toss my blanket over my legs, then I push back so the recliner is activated. The best thing I ever did was pay extra to have extra sectional sections added to this couch.

Best. Thing. Ever.

Flynn laughs. "Getting comfy, are we?"

"Yes. Yes, I am. Your seat has a recliner too, ya know," I say with a big smile.

"Awesome." He reaches to the side and pushes the button so his recliner comes out as well.

We're sitting so close that our thighs and arms are touching, and that has me feeling all sorts of things. Heat. Passion. Want. Need. All things I shouldn't feel for a stranger I just met, but here I am. Feeling. And wanting. Wanting so freaking badly.

He slides his hand onto my thigh. "So . . . are we ready?"

His touch is like fire, and it feels as if his hand may burn a hole into my thigh. It may be too warm for this blanket.

I take a deep breath, then blow it out. "Yes. I'm ready." Flynn stifles a giggle as he hits play on the remote.

Chapter 7

Flynn

This was a bad idea. I should have known better than to show up here. But I couldn't help it. I needed to get out of my hotel and try to do some thinking, so I went out for a walk. I shouldn't have been surprised when that walk led me right to Delaney's front stoop. I've been thinking about her nonstop since I first saw her at the coffee shop two days ago. I thought about turning around and going right back to my hotel, but I figured a quick text message wouldn't hurt, so I reached out. I was shocked when she answered so quickly. I was partly hoping she wasn't going to answer, because then I could have gone back to the hotel—probably would have been less trouble. But she did. And now I'm inside her house, sitting right next to her on this extremely comfortable couch, trying to watch a movie.

Easier said than done.

Being this close to her has my mind all sorts of fucked up and fuzzy. All I can think about is kissing the fuck out of her. And I would, but I shouldn't be thinking about that. What I should be thinking about is telling her who I am. The longer I wait, the worse it's going to be. But I know there's a very good chance that she's going to tell me to get the fuck out when I finally do come clean, and I'm not ready for everything to end yet.

I suck, I know.

I close my eyes and take a deep breath. I can't help but be very aware of the fact that her body is pressed up against mine and it's basically calling to me. At this very moment, I want nothing more than to carry her ass to her bedroom, peel her clothes off, and make love to her and do all sorts of things to her. But I can't do that.

I take another deep breath and try to relax. I really am trying, but I can't focus on the movie. I can't focus on anything besides the fact that Delaney's leg is touching mine and my hand is still on her thigh. I need the pizza to get here—right now. Because all I can think about is sliding my hand higher up her thigh.

"Do you want to talk?" she asks, breaking the silence.

Dear God, yes. Get my mind focused on something else.

"I know we're here to watch a movie, but it wouldn't be a bad thing to talk a little while we wait for the pizza," I agree, and I pause the movie. "What do you want to know?"

Be careful, dude. Be very careful.

"You said you're thirty years old. Do you have any siblings?"

"Nope, just me. How about you? Any siblings other than your brother?"

"Twin brother. And no, it's just us."

"Twins, huh? That's pretty cool."

"Yeah. It's pretty awesome being a twin, but it's even more awesome that my twin is a boy. It was nice knowing that I'd always have someone there to watch my back and kick the crap out of someone if need be when we were younger," she replies with a smile.

I'm definitely getting my ass beat for this.

"Uh, nice," I say with a chuckle. "What's your brother's name?"

"Dylan," Delaney replies.

"Nice. Do you have any more family here?"

Way to sound like a creeper.

"I do. My parents still live here, and I also have two cousins in town."

I definitely didn't think this through.

"Wow. Must be nice to have your family close."

"Yeah. We have a huge gathering for Christmas every year. It's massive."

"I remember."

"What?" she asks, almost alarmed.

Holy fuck.

I fake a cough before I continue, "Sorry. I remember gatherings like those. I miss doing stuff like that."

Holy fuck, I almost blew it.

"I know what you mean. With my brother in Italy, we haven't had a full gathering in a while, but that'll change since he's coming home."

Fuck. Me.

"Your brother is coming home? That's awesome!" I reply, trying to sound convincing.

"Yeah, he texted me earlier and told me he'll be home for a few days. I'm super excited!"

"I bet. Can I use your bathroom?"

"Yes, of course. Down the hall, first door on your right."

"Thanks," I reply, getting up off the couch.

Not only do I have to take a leak, but I need a minute or two to breathe and calm myself the fuck down. I walk down the hall, then go into the bathroom and close and lock the door. I quickly take a leak, then wash my hands, but I don't exit the bathroom right away. I stand at the sink and look at myself in the mirror.

This was such a bad idea. What the fuck were you thinking?

I stay in the bathroom a few more minutes, then take a deep breath before I exit and walk back down the hall to the living room. Delaney is still sitting on the couch, but she's looking down at her lap. I'm about to ask if she's okay, but then I notice that she has her cell phone in her hand.

"Everything okay?" I ask as I sit next to her.

"Yes. Everything is fine."

"Do you want to turn the movie back on now?" I ask, praying she says yes.

Talking leaves too many opportunities for me to fuck up and blow myself up. Also, Dylan coming home complicates everything. I didn't tell him I was coming to visit Delaney when we talked a few weeks ago. Hell, I didn't mention coming here at all because I didn't want him to know. I know he would have called Delaney and that would have been the end of that. Plus, he probably would have threatened my ass.

And rightfully so.

"Sure. As long as you'll protect me," she says sweetly.

I don't answer right away, and I feel her tense next to me a little.

Fuck. Get it together, ya pussy.

"Of course I will," I reply, pressing play.

Delaney snuggles against me, and within a few moments, I'm right back to where I was before I went to the bathroom. Delaney is pressed up against me, and I can't stop thinking about doing bad things to her.

Jesus. When did I become so whipped?

I do my best to focus on the movie, and I can't help but chuckle whenever Delaney jumps during the scary parts. I won't say anything out loud because I don't want to embarrass her, but I about fucking died when she jumped and her hand landed dangerously close to my dick. I was trying so hard to keep him calm, but that definitely woke him up. For the millionth time since I got here, I think about what a bad idea this was.

I glance down at Delaney, and it seems like she isn't affected by how close we are sitting like I am. Either that or she is damn good at hiding it. And if that's the case, I should bow down to the master.

"So, what are you here for?" Delaney suddenly asks.

Oh no . . .

"What do you mean?" I ask, pausing the movie again.

Watching a movie tonight probably wasn't the best idea. She did say I felt familiar to her, but she doesn't know why. As far as she knows, I could be a crazy person. But here I am.

"Well, you said you're staying at the hotel, which means you don't live here. So why are you here?"

"Oh, uh . . . I'm here for work meetings and such."

"What do you do for work?"

Damn is she an inquisitive little monkey tonight.

"I work in a corporate office. What about you? What do you do?"

Not a total lie, but I definitely need to get the spotlight off me before I do or say something wrong again.

"My family owns the Lakeview B&B. I've been an assistant manager there for a few years. I'm on vacation right now."

I already knew that, but it would have seemed weird if I didn't ask.

"That's pretty awesome," I reply.

"Yeah," Delaney says, and she snuggles back into my side again.

I did it. I survived the questions. Maybe I'll be okay.

Chapter 8

Delaney

I am dying. Literally dying.

Having Flynn pressed up against my side is pure torture. I started talking and asking questions, because not only was I getting more and more nervous but also I really want to know more about him. He seems so calm and unbothered by the fact that we are pressed up against one another, and it actually makes me feel a little uneasy. Like maybe he doesn't like me the same way I like him so far.

I don't want to seem like a creeper, but every once in a while, I sneak a peek in his direction to see if he looks like he is struggling like I am. He looks calm for a little bit, but then his posture begins to change. I sneak another peek a few minutes later and finally, his face says everything. I can tell by how tense he is that this is hard for him as well. I lean forward and grab my glass and take a small sip. I haven't eaten since this morning, so this wine is going to go to my head really fast. I need to take it slow so I don't make an ass out of myself.

We are about thirty minutes into the movie when the doorbell finally rings.

"Oh, thank goodness!" I blurt out. "I mean . . . I'm starving."

Flynn laughs as he reaches for the remote to pause the movie. I stand and toss my blanket onto the other end of the couch as I walk toward the door. I stop and grab my wallet out of my purse, then unlock the door and pull open the door. I pay for the pizza, then close and lock the door before returning to the couch. Then I run to the kitchen and grab some paper plates.

"We're using my finest china tonight. I hope you don't mind," I say with a giggle as I hand a paper plate to Flynn.

He laughs, then takes the plate from me. "This is my favorite kind of plate. Very low maintenance." He grabs the remote and turns the movie back on.

We eat our pizza, drink our wine, and continue watching the movie. I try my hardest not to jump, but I do quite a few times. Flynn doesn't laugh at me, instead he just pulls me closer. Once we're done with our pizza, he full-on holds me. Having his arms around me feels amazing—there is no other way to describe it. I feel like I'm meant to be here with him. By the time the movie is over, I'm totally freaked out, but I'm not going to let Flynn see that. Not wanting to move a muscle, I snuggle into his chest and close my eyes. I could probably fall asleep right here in his arms.

"How you holding up?" Flynn asks after a few moments of silence.

I open my eyes and look up at him. "Honestly?"

"Yes."

"Well . . ." I play with the fabric of his shirt. "I'm scared shitless," I say in a dead-serious tone.

Flynn chuckles and tightens his arms around me. "Yes, I can tell. I was going to ask if you wanted to watch part two, but I'm thinking that isn't such a good idea."

I snuggle my head back to his chest before I answer. "Not unless you want to spend the night and protect me," I say, then wait for his reply.

Flynn doesn't answer, and I'm worried I might have said too much. I lean back and look up at him, and the look on his face is so intense.

"Delaney . . . I would love to stay the night and protect you. But—" Flynn says, then stops.

I do my best to hide the disappointment I'm sure is written all over my face.

"I know. It was a silly question. I was just kidding anyway," I say quickly, then stand. "Would you like some more wine?" I ask, walking toward the kitchen.

I only manage to get a few steps before Flynn wraps his arms around me and pulls me back against his firm chest.

"I was going to say, *but* I have an early meeting tomorrow. I'd have to be up and out of here by five a.m. That way, I have time to get back to my hotel and get showered and dressed," he says, still holding me in place.

"No, I totally get it. What kind of meeting is it?"

It's none of my business, really, but I want to know more about him.

"There isn't much I can tell you about my work, Delaney. I am here checking some things out, and depending on how this visit goes, my visit might become permanent," he says, but stops.

Before I can say another word, he leans down and crashes his lips to mine. The amount of passion and fire I feel behind this kiss has my mind going completely foggy. I seem to completely forget that I've known this man for less than two days. But none of that matters at this moment. All that matters is me and him, and the passion we are clearly both feeling. I pull back and look at Flynn for a moment. His cheeks are slightly red, his eyes are dark, and he's breathing heavily. I want nothing more than to take this man to my bed right now. And I have just about enough wine in my system to allow myself to act without thinking about it.

I pull out of Flynn's grasp, then walk back toward the table and grab my wineglass, quickly chugging whatever is left. Then I grab Flynn's glass and do the same.

"What the hell are you doing?" he asks.

I walk back toward Flynn, then throw my arms around his neck. "Liquid courage," I say, before I lean up and kiss him.

"Liquid courage, huh?" he asks with a chuckle.

"Yes. I am not the type of woman who makes a move, ever. But I'm a completely different woman with wine in my system."

"Ah. I see. Are you telling me that you're getting drunk, Del?" Flynn asks seriously.

"A little bit," I reply with a giggle as I lean up and place some kisses on his neck.

He's tense at first, but he quickly relaxes before he slides his hands onto my hips and hoists me up. I don't have time to feel insecure about him picking me up, so I just go with it. I wrap my legs around Flynn's waist, and he slides his arms around me as he continues the assault on my lips.

"Bedroom. Where?" Flynn asks, pulling his lips from mine.

"Down the hall," I reply before I kiss him again.

Flynn starts moving through the house, heading toward my bedroom. He walks into my room, then carefully sets me down. I back up slowly so I'm a few feet from him. I am so turned on and want him so badly. I know I'm giving him my "fuck me" eyes, and he seems to be loving it.

Flynn watches as I slowly unzip my hoodie. I pull it off and drop it onto the floor near the end of the bed. Then I pull my tank top over my head and drop it in the same spot. I slip my thumbs into the waistband of my yoga pants next. Flynn closes the distance between us in two steps and stops me as I'm about to slide down my pants.

"Are you sure? We don't have to do this tonight," he says.

I smile up at him. "I've never been more sure of anything in my entire life," I reply as I push my leggings down my legs.

They pool at my feet, and I glance up at Flynn to see his reaction. He growls and licks his bottom lip and then he is on me again, crashing his lips to mine. He reaches around my back and unclasps my bra. Once it's off, he tosses it to the floor, then he slides his fingers into the waistband of my panties. He breaks our kiss as he slides my panties down. His face comes so close to my core, and I suck in a breath as soon as I feel his breath on me. He places a gentle kiss just below my belly button, then stands.

"You have too many clothes on," I say innocently, reaching for the zipper on Flynn's hoodie.

He smacks my hand away, and for a moment, I'm kind of shocked. I wonder if maybe I'm moving too fast. I lean down and reach for my hoodie, but Flynn stops me.

"Don't you dare. Go sit on the bed."

Flynn's gaze is so heated that I don't dare question him. I am so completely turned-= on right now, and I can feel how heated my cheeks are. I lightly bite my lower lip and that gets me another growl.

"Bed. Now, Delaney," he says, and I shiver at his tone.

Flynn's eyes don't leave me as I walk over to the bed. I plop down, which makes my tits bounce a little. I am usually quite self-conscious, but in this moment, I couldn't care less that I am buck naked. I don't even need to ask Flynn how he's feeling—it's written all over his face. My gaze travels down the length of his body, and I see that it's also written somewhere else. The bulge in his pants says exactly how turned on he really is. He stares at me like he wants to devour me, but he doesn't say a word and he hasn't moved.

"Flynn . . . ? Are you okay?" I ask, concerned.

"I . . ."

"What is it?"

"I'm so sorry, Delaney. I can't do this," he says before he turns and bolts out of my room.

I sit there in complete disbelief. I feel like I've just been smacked in the face. I can't believe I am sitting here completely naked, and he just bolted. I don't understand what happened. I quickly grab my pants and tank top off the floor and put them on before I storm out of my room. I'm about to start screaming and cursing like a sailor, but I'm shocked to find that my living room is already empty.

Wait a second . . . What the hell just happened?!

Chapter 9

Flynn

I wake up the next morning and feel even more like a piece of shit than I did when I finally went to bed last night. Delaney blew up my phone for a while with extremely hurt text messages, which turned into pissed off messages, and I don't blame her one bit. I wanted to do it; I wanted to make love to her. But as I stood there looking at her completely naked and waiting for me, I realized it would be a complete betrayal if I had sex with her before I told her who I really am. So I took the coward's way out and bolted. I didn't even put my shoes or coat on. I just grabbed everything and ran out the front door. And I didn't stop until I got a few houses away.

I fucking suck.

I grab my phone off the nightstand, then open Delaney's text thread and reread all of her messages from last night.

Did I do something wrong?

I don't understand what happened.

Why won't you talk to me?

What did I do to deserve that?

Flynn! Talk to me, dammit!

YA KNOW WHAT? FUCK YOU!

I reread the last message a few times, then toss my phone onto the bed next to me. I really fucked up. There is no way she'll forgive me after last night. I might as well pack my shit now and leave town, cause there is no point in staying.

My phone chimes again, so I reach down and prepare myself for another verbal beating. Which I totally deserve.

Hey, brother! I'm coming home for a few days. Was wondering where you're living now and if you'd have time to meet up?

Fuck me!

Dylan will beat the ever-loving shit out of me if he finds out what happened last night. Now I definitely don't have a choice. I have to get out of here before he comes home.

Hey D. That would be awesome, but I'm nowhere near North Shore.

I really am going straight to hell. I should have just told Delaney from the beginning. Lying to her, and now to Dylan, is just plain ole fucked up.

When did I become this shitty fucking man?

Where are you? Maybe we can still meet up before I go back.

I'm on assignment for work, so I probably won't be able to.

Okay. Is everything okay, dude?

Yeah. Everything is great.

I am such a liar. What the hell is wrong with me?

Okay. Just thought it would be nice to meet up and grab a beer or something. It's been years.

I know. And I appreciate it. Just have a lot going on right now.

Understatement of the fucking year!

Okay. If you're sure.

I should reply. I should say something, anything. Dylan is my fucking best friend, and I'm blowing him off because I made a huge mess of this and I know he's going to kick the shit out of me once he sees me. I need to pack my shit and go back home and forget all about this weekend and Delaney. I think things could have been different if I had just come clean at the very beginning. But now I'm way too deep in my own lie. I don't think there's any way Delaney will ever forgive me, nor do I think Dylan will forgive me when he finds out. Hell, I don't deserve their forgiveness. Not now, not ever.

I decide to stay in bed for a little longer, but I finally get up a little after eight-thirty and get my suitcase out of the closet. I start shoving all my clothes in, then walk into the bathroom. I quickly take a piss, then wash my hands before I start grabbing the little bit of stuff I'm taking home with me. I'm actually paid up for another week, but I think it would be best to just leave now. I'm standing at the bed finishing up my packing when there's a knock at my door.

Who the hell could that be?

I walk over to the door and pull it open without looking through the peephole first.

Goddamnit.

"Delaney . . . What are you doing here?" I ask, surprised.

"I'm not sure, to be honest."

"How did you know what room I was in?"

Delaney doesn't say anything for a few moments and neither do I. She just stares at me, and I know what's about to come. I wouldn't be a bit surprised if I get my ass beat by her.

"Do you want to come in?"

"No."

"Do you want to talk?"

"No. Yes . . . I don't know."

"If you're not sure, then what are you doing here?"

"I don't know. I guess I just had to come see you and stare you down. Now that I know who you are. Flynn Michael Westin."

Fuck.

"How did you—"

"I have friends who work here," she snaps.

"Oh."

Now would be a really good time to apologize and beg for her forgiveness. Then I should try to explain why I did what I did—not that there is any excusable reason. But I can't seem to get the words out. Quite frankly, I can't even meet her gaze right now.

"I was talking about the guy I met and liked, and I mentioned your name and that you were staying here. One of my friends chimed in and said she had checked you in. And then she said your last name just to verify that we were talking about the same Flynn."

I finally look up and instantly wish I hadn't. Delaney's beautiful eyes are full of tears, and I want to kick my own ass right now.

"Delaney, I—"

"Don't."

"Please let me—"

"*No*! How could you not tell me? We haven't seen each other in *years*. We were kids! You had to know I wouldn't recognize you. Why wouldn't you tell me?!"

"Delaney, please—"

"No! Do not 'Delaney, please' me! Why would you do this? Was this all just a game to you?"

"No! This wasn't a game to me. Not in the slightest. I didn't mean for this to happen."

"You didn't mean for what to happen? You didn't mean to show up and not tell me who you were? You didn't mean to come back into my life, get close to me, and make me like you? You didn't mean to come to my house and damn near fuck me?"

"Delaney, please," I beg.

I've never begged anyone for anything in my entire life, but I need to beg now. I dug this hole that I'm in, and I need to figure out how—and if—I can get myself out of it.

"Have you talked to Dylan? Does he know you're here?"

"We've talked, but no, he doesn't know I'm here."

Delaney scoffs, then closes her eyes. She's visibly shaking, and I want nothing more than to pull her against my chest and hold her until she forgives me, no matter how long it takes.

"Delaney, please. I'm so fucking sorry. I never meant for this to go this far. I just wanted to see you, talk to you. I wanted you to see me—as an adult, as a man. Not just as your brother's best friend."

Delaney finally opens her eyes, and the tears start spilling down her cheeks.

Fuck. Fuck. Fuck.

"You didn't even give me a chance to get to know you as an adult. You just started lying right off the bat. What kind of person does that?"

An asshole, that's the kind of person who does that.

"I know, and I'm so sorry. I thought you would turn me away because of my friendship with your brother."

"So instead you lied? What is wrong with you?!"

I drop my gaze to the floor. I'm so ashamed I can't even look Delaney in the eye anymore.

"I'm so sorry," I reply sadly.

"I don't ever want to see you again, Flynn. Not ever."

"Please don't say that. You don't mean it," I reply, forcing myself to look back up.

"I do mean it. You have no idea how much I mean it. Lose my phone number and don't ever come back."

"Delaney—"

"Goodbye, Flynn," she says before she turns and walks down the hallway toward the elevator.

What the fuck have I done?

Chapter 10

Delaney

I try so hard to keep my composure as I make my way to the elevator, but what I really want to do is break down. I feel so empty right now. I don't even know what to say or do. I hadn't seen Flynn in almost twenty years, so of course, I didn't recognize him. But he sought me out; he knew who I was. He fed me bullshit about being in town for work. I believed he was a good guy, and he liked me. Come to find out he's the guy I've been in love with since I was younger. To me, he was always the one who got away. I never got to tell him how I felt. Partly because of his friendship with my brother, and partly because I was scared of being rejected. I don't understand why he would do this to me.

I finally reach the elevator, and I hit the down button and wait. Flynn is still standing in the hallway watching me. I know he is—I can feel it. I had to walk away. I couldn't stand there anymore. I wanted to slap him. Punch him. Hug him. Kiss him. I'm so beyond confused. I have no idea what I did to him to make him play this cruel prank on me.

The elevator finally opens, and I step inside. As soon as the doors shut, I close my eyes and try to breathe through the emotion that is threatening to spill out. I need to get home, and I need to talk to Joy. My phone chimes in my pocket and I'm tempted to see who it is, but I'm almost afraid to. It's probably Flynn. I finally open my eyes in time for the doors to open again, so I step out into the lobby and quickly make my way toward the front doors. Thankfully, I don't see anyone I know, so

I'm able to rush right out of the hotel without any interruptions. Once outside, I rush down the front steps, then make my way home. It's only a little after eight in the morning, and it's very cold, so there aren't many people out and about right now.

Thank God.

I don't think I could handle having to talk to anyone right now. I'm barely keeping the tears back at this point. I just want to get home, then I can deal with the breakdown that is on its way. I pull my phone from my pocket and pull up Joy's text thread.

I need you. Please come to my house ASAP.

Thanks to my speed walking, I make it home in record time. I get inside and start pulling my winter layers off when the tears begin falling with a vengeance. I'm crying so hard that I can't even see what the hell I'm doing, so I leave my layers by the door and make my way to the couch. I lay down and pull the blanket on top of me and let everything out.

I knew there was something familiar about Flynn, but I didn't stop and question it like I should have. Come to think of it, I never even asked his last name. I just let him into my home, into my life, into my heart. He was very wrong for not immediately telling me who he was, but I am also in the wrong. I never should've let him into my life without asking more questions. I was just so overwhelmed by how he made me feel that I never even questioned it, or questioned him. And now I have to deal with the consequences of my actions.

My phone chimes so I quickly grab it and see that there is one messages from Joy and one from Flynn. I open Joy's message because I don't think I have it in me to read what Flynn wrote right now.

I'm on my way! What happened?! Are you okay?

Joy and I have both had each other's backs through numerous break-ups over the years, and I couldn't be more thankful for our friendship. Joy is definitely the sister I never had, and I can't imagine my life without her.

I stare at my phone. I really want to check my message from Flynn. I want to see what else he had to say to me. I am mortified over the fact that I didn't recognize him, but I am more mortified over the fact that he considered having sex with me before he even told me who he was. What kind of person does something like that? I take a deep breath and try to calm myself, but as soon as I think about what happened last night, I get ridiculously upset and the tears begin spilling down my cheeks once again.

I must cry myself to sleep because the next thing I remember is Joy waking me up.

"Delaney . . . are you okay?"

"No," I reply honestly.

"What happened? Are your parents okay? Your brother?"

"They're fine," I whisper.

"Then what happened? This isn't like you, Del."

"Flynn," I whisper.

"Flynn did this?! I'll kill him! What did he do, Del?"

I want to respond, but I can't. I know I'm going to lose it as soon as I say what happened. Instead, I stand and walk over to my mantle and grab the picture of Flynn, Dylan, and me, then I make my way back to the couch. I sit next to Joy and hand her the picture.

"I don't understand," she says.

I take a deep breath and try to calm myself before I speak.

"That is me, Dylan, and his best friend Flynn. This was taken the day Flynn and his parents moved away. We were thirteen."

"Okay . . . ?"

"Flynn Michael Westin."

"Del, I don't understand. What does this picture have to do with why you're so upset?"

I close my eyes and take a deep breath, then open them. "The little boy in this picture . . . ? He came back into my life."

"What?"

"At the coffee shop. And then again on Friday, when I was on a date with the idiot . . . "

I watch as Joy puts two and two together and realization smacks her in the face.

"Oh. My. God!" she yells.

"Yeah . . . " I reply, getting emotional again.

"Wait! Are you telling me that this boy—this Flynn—is the same Flynn you met the other night? The one who rescued you from your blind date from hell?"

"Yeah."

"The one who came over last night and had you naked in your room?!"

As soon as Joy says those words, the waterworks turn on again and I begin bawling. I am so embarrassed, angry, upset, and overwhelmed that I don't know what to do.

"Oh my god, Delaney. I am so sorry!" Joy says, wrapping her arms around me.

She holds me and lets me cry until I feel like I can't cry anymore. By the time I pull away, my eyes hurt and my nose is a solid block of snot.

Very attractive, I know.

"Del, what are you going to do?" Joy finally asks.

"I went to his hotel and confronted him. I yelled at him and told him to lose my number. Then I said I don't ever want to see him again," I whisper.

"Wow. What did he say?"

"That he didn't mean for this to happen, and that he's sorry. Blah, blah, blah."

"Wow. Does your brother know?"

"I don't think so."

"You have to tell Dylan."

"I can't. He'll kick the fuck out of Flynn."

And that's the truth. If Dylan finds out Flynn came here and got close to me and didn't tell me who he was, Dylan will find him and beat the shit out of Flynn. They might be best friends, but I'm his sister. Blood is thicker than water.

"I know. And he fucking deserves it!"

"I can't let that happen, Joy."

"Why the fuck not?!"

I stand and start pacing back and forth. I should let Dylan kick the crap out of Flynn, but I'm not like that. I would never intentionally cause someone harm. Plus, there's the reason that I've been trying to avoid since I found out who he is. I stop pacing and turn to face Joy.

"I can't because I've been in love with him since I was twelve years old. No matter how badly he hurt me, I can't let Dylan beat the shit out of him."

"Jesus, Del. I'm so sorry this happened. What are you going to do?"

No clue.

"Try to forget about Flynn, I suppose. Move on and put this bullshit behind me," I reply.

Truth be told, I have no idea if I'm going to be able to put this behind me. I started to realize how much I actually liked Flynn when I was around twelve years old, and I just turned thirty-one. It's been nineteen years, and I'm still crazy about him. I didn't even know a twelve-year-old could fall in love with someone, but clearly, I did. I have no idea how I'm going to get him out of my system.

"He texted me, ya know," I whisper sadly.

"What did he say?"

"I didn't even read his message."

"Are you going to?"

"I don't know. Should I?"

"I can't tell you what to do, Del. If it was me, I would probably be out for blood. But this isn't just some random Joe Shmoe. This is your brother's best friend. It's a completely different ballgame."

I don't say anything right away because I'm not really sure what to say. Part of me wants to see what he has to say for himself, but the other part of me is scared to see what he has to say. I walk back over to the couch and sit next to Joy, then grab my phone off the table.

"I think I need to see what he said."

"Okay, then do it. I won't look if you don't want me to, but I'm right here."

I nod at Joy, then unlock my phone and open Flynn's text thread.

Here we go . . .

I know I fucked this up. So badly. And I am so fucking sorry, Delaney. I was scared to tell you who I really was because I didn't want you to just dismiss me because I'm Dylan's best friend. I'm so sorry I hurt you.

"So?" Joy asks after a few minutes of silence.

"He said he fucked up, and he's so sorry, and he was afraid I was going to dismiss him."

Joy shakes her head. "That doesn't make any sense."

"No . . . It kinda does."

"What are you talking about?"

"He was Dylan's best friend, which made him untouchable. I never would have considered anything with him."

"So he lied to you? Delaney . . . that's bullshit."

"No, you're right. I kind of understand why he did what he did, but that doesn't excuse the fact that he did it," I reply sadly.

Joy gets up and walks into the kitchen, then comes back a few minutes later with two cups of coffee.

"Here. Coffee always fixes everything," Joy says, handing me a cup.

"Thanks," I reply with a sniffle.

Chapter 11

Delaney

J oy tries to cheer me up, but it doesn't really work. I'm feeling so many emotions today, and I kind of just don't want to be bothered. I know I called her over, but I feel like I'm in such a funk right now, and that's not good for anybody.

"I think I'm going to head out now, Del. I have to get to work in a little bit," Joy says after about two hours.

"Okay. I'm sorry I kept you."

"Are you kidding? You're my best friend. You know I would stay if I could, but Christmas is right around the corner, and I have to make sure everything is on schedule."

Fuck. I completely forgot Christmas is next week. And my brother is coming home too.

"I want you to call me if you need anything else. Okay?"

"Sure," I reply, pulling my dead ass off the couch.

Joy pulls me into a big hug, and she holds me longer than she needs to, but the comfort right now feels amazing. Though I do have to admit, I wish the comfort was coming from someone else.

"I love you, bestie," Joy says with a smile as she pulls back.

"Love you too."

Joy walks toward the front door, then pulls her coat on. She turns and smiles at me once more before she opens the door and heads back out into the freezing morning.

It's hard to believe that it's only a little before eleven in the morning and I'm already so exhausted. But I guess that's what happens when you stay up really late angry-texting and crying, and then have a shitty night's sleep once you do go to bed.

I make sure to lock the door after Joy leaves, then I walk back over to the couch and collapse on it. I pull the blanket down from the back of the couch and close my eyes, wishing more than anything that some sleep will come. Unfortunately, all I can think about is Flynn. I feel so hurt, upset, angry, betrayed, and just completely broken. Even though he was a kid then, the Flynn I knew years ago was smart and kind, and I can't imagine he would have ever done something so malicious. But I hadn't seen that him in over twenty years, so I really have no idea who he is anymore.

I consider texting my brother and telling him what happened, but with him coming home in a few days, I know it is a very bad idea to tell him. He was always super protective of me, even as kids, and I wouldn't put it past him to beat Flynn within an inch of his life over this bullshit. Quite frankly, I kind of feel like I'm protecting Flynn and Dylan by not telling Dylan what happened. I don't really want my brother to go to jail, nor do I want Flynn to be dead.

I grab my cell phone off the table and pull up Flynn's text thread. I know I should just forget about him, but I've never been known to just roll over and play dead, so to speak. I might have told him face-to-face that I never want to see him again, and that's exactly how I feel, but I haven't gotten to yell at him via text message yet, and I'm feeling feisty enough to do it right now.

I don't understand how you could do something like this to me, Flynn. Do you hate me so much that you felt like you had to completely humiliate me?

I feel strong when I hit send, but then as I wait for a response, I start to feel stupid for messaging him. I quickly get up off the couch and walk into the kitchen. I've had exotic fruit wine in my refrigerator for three weeks, and I've yet to drink any of it. At this moment, I don't give a shit that it's not even noon yet. I think I need a little alcohol in my system in case he does answer my message.

I quickly open the bottle, then take one of my eighteen-ounce wine-glasses from the top of my cabinet and fill it to the rim. Considering the fact that I've barely slept, I haven't eaten, and I'm in a terrible mood, I know this alcohol is going to go straight to my head, but I really don't give a shit. I take a few sips so it is low enough that I can carry it to the living room, then I set the glass down on the table by the couch. I sit back down on the couch and pull the blanket over me, then check my phone. There are no messages yet, so I put my phone down on the sofa arm and pick up the glass and take a long drink.

I'm not really a lightweight, but I swear I can feel the alcohol hitting my system already. I really should get something to eat while I drink, but I am in such a shitty mood right now that I really don't care. I don't care if I say something asshole-ish to Flynn because he fucking deserves it. He approached me and didn't tell me who he was. He came to my house and didn't tell me who he was. We were talking about our lives and he didn't tell me who he was. He had me naked in my bedroom, and still, he didn't tell me who he was. The only thing more betraying than all of that would be if he had actually slept with me. And I have to admit, if that had happened, I definitely would've told Dylan about it, and I definitely would've let him kill Flynn.

The more I think about it, the more pissed off I get. I grab my glass off the table and take a long drink again. It's probably a good thing that I'm on vacation from work right now because drinking this wine this fast is not going to be pretty later. But then again, I'm an adult, I am extremely pissed off, and I really don't give a shit.

I'm about to finish my first glass of wine when my phone chimes. My heart skips a beat and I'm actually quite annoyed. I don't know if it's because I'm worried that it's Flynn or if I'm excited that it could be Flynn. What I do know is that I should not be excited that he is texting me. I have to make sure I remember that he betrayed me and he does not deserve to be forgiven.

I take a deep breath, then pick up my phone and check my notifications. Flynn's name appears, but I don't open the message right away. I just kind of stare for a couple of moments, then I take another deep breath and open his text thread.

I do not hate you. I never hated you. Ever. I never meant for this to happen. I'm not trying to make excuses for what I did, but it had been so long since we've seen each other, and I didn't want you to remember me as your brother's best friend. I wanted you to get to know me as the man I am now. And I am so fucking sorry for what I did.

Well, I would say I got to know you as the man you are today. And quite frankly, I don't think I like the man you've become. I don't think I've ever met a man who would do what you did. Do you not have a conscience?

It might be harsh, but he deserves every mean word I can possibly give him. And if I'm being completely honest, me giving him some harsh words is much better than the ass whooping he would be getting if I told my brother what happened.

Text bubbles appear and stay there for a few seconds before they disappear, but no message comes. I wonder if he's changed his mind about answering, and that might be for the best. He might be Dylan's best friend, but I don't see any reason why I should continue to talk to or try to be friends with him—not that I would want that after what he did.

I pull myself up off the couch and grab my wine glass, then walk into the kitchen. I empty the bottle into my glass, then pick it up and take another drink before I make my way back to the couch. My phone chimes just as I sit down, and I contemplate whether I want to see who it is. I think about it as best I can, but in the end, I finally decide I need to see what he said, if that's who messaged me. I take a long sip of wine, then put my glass on the table and pick up my phone. I take a deep breath, then flip it over.

It's from him.

I know I didn't handle this right. At all. And you have every right to be pissed off at me, but please, don't think I don't have a conscience. Because I do. And I feel terrible. Truly terrible.

You're damn right I have every right to be pissed off. I'm actually more than pissed off; livid is a good word for how I'm feeling.

Good. You should feel terrible.

I do.

I just have one question. One. Simple. Question.

Ask me. Anything.

How could you not tell me? I mean . . . I don't understand. You talk like you care about me. But if you really did care, then you never would have pulled what you did.

I'm getting angrier as the seconds pass, but it's not just anger that's there—it's hurt. I'm so hurt that he lied to me. Hurt that he got me to like him. Hurt that he saw me naked. Hurt that he walked away like he did.

I grab my glass and drain it again. All this alcohol in a short period of time isn't going to be a good thing, but I don't care right now. I need something to keep me going, and I don't think coffee would do it for me.

I was scared.

Scared of what?! You're a big, strong dude. What the hell could you have been scared of?

Little text bubbles appear, but then they disappear, and another message doesn't come.

"Ugh, whatever!" I yell, tossing my phone onto the other couch.

I get up and stomp into the kitchen and grab another bottle of wine out of my fridge. It takes me a few minutes to get the damn thing open, but once I do, I stomp my way back to the couch and plop down with the bottle in my hand. I grab the TV remote, turn on my favorite tornado show, and get comfortable. I attempt to focus on my show for a good thirty minutes, I really do. But I start to realize that my vision is going funky, and my lips are kind of numb. I know what that means. I am bordering on shit-faced . . . possibly on my way to being beyond shit-faced. I'm smashed. And I have to pee. Which is terrible. To me, peeing is also called breaking the seal. And breaking the seal usually makes me more drunk, which makes absolutely no sense, but it's true.

My phone chimes again, and I give it the side-eye as I take a big gulp of wine from the bottle. I try to focus on the TV, but I'm pretty much wasted, and I know there's no way I'm going to be able to pay attention. I put the bottle of wine on the table and get up. I instantly regret the decision when the room starts to spin.

"Whoa," I say with a giggle.

I make my way to the other couch, then plop down and grab my phone. I open Flynn's message, then close one eye and do the best I can to read what it says.

Scared that you were going to turn me away because of my friendship with your brother. Scared that you wouldn't even give me a chance.

I'm soooooooodrink. Deunk. Drunk. Hahahahaha.

What did you drink?

Idranklotsofwpne

Delaney . . . Are you home alone?

Wny? You donte care.

Please answer me. Are you alone?

Whyditoucare?!

Of course, I'm alone! You're not here. Because you're an ass, and you played me.

Delaney . . . please.

Delaney?

I don't respond. Instead, I lay my head against the armrest of the couch. The room spins around me, and I legit can't even see straight. I close my eyes in hopes that the spinning stops but that doesn't seem to help. The spinning continues only in the dark this time.

Ugh. Great.

Chapter 12

Flynn

I stare at my phone and wait for a response, but nothing comes. I've seen drunk texting before, but Delaney's messages were on a whole other level of fucked up, and now I'm more than just a little bit worried about her. Drunk is one thing, but upset, pissed off, and drunk . . . ? That's a bad combination.

I consider the possibilities of what to do. If I text her brother, he's going to know I'm here and he will probably call me and verbally kick my ass. Plus, there's really nothing he can do from Italy anyway. I don't know her best friend's phone number, so I can't ask her to check on Delaney. I can't go to her parents' house and ask them to check on her. Nothing seems good enough. The only thing that is even remotely acceptable is for me to go over and check on her myself. But even that comes with its own issues. She doesn't want to see me, and I don't know if I can look her in the eye again. I'm too ashamed of what I let happen. But the idea of not checking on her isn't acceptable either. If anything were to happen to her, I would never forgive myself. I pick up my phone and send her another message in hopes that she'll answer.

Delaney . . . I know you hate me right now, but please just let me know you are okay. Please.

Dammit, Delaney, come on.

Five minutes pass and she still doesn't answer, so I get up and walk toward my suitcase, which is still sitting on the bed. I pull out jeans and a hoodie and quickly get changed. Five minutes later, I throw my coat and boots on and grab my keycard off the table, then head out the door. I don't give a shit if she gets even more mad at me; I have to check on her and make sure she's okay.

I get into the elevator when my phone chimes in my pocket. I quickly pull it out and see Dylan's name, so I unlock my phone and check the message.

Hey. So I have a question for you.

What's up?

Why did you tell me you're not in North Shore? I know you're there right now.

Fuck. Me.

What are you talking about?

I'm so fucked right now.

Come on, dude.

No point in denying it anymore. He already knows I'm here.

How'd you find out?

The elevator doors open, and I step out into the hotel lobby. My phone chimes again so I stop walking and check my phone.

Mom saw you walking toward the hotel. Why didn't you tell me you were home, dude?

He doesn't know why I'm here. Just that I'm here.

It wasn't a planned trip. I just kind of found myself here.

How long are you staying for? I'll be home on Wednesday. Let's meet up.

Maybe. I'm not sure if I'll still be here.

I slip my phone back into my pocket, then quickly walk across the lobby and out the front door. Within a few minutes, I'm standing outside of Delaney's place. Her car is in the driveway and there's no other cars here, so she must be alone. Unless someone walked. But I don't really care. I need to see her. I need to make sure she is okay.

Here we go.

I walk up Delaney's front steps and knock on the door a few times. When she doesn't answer, I start looking around for a hide-a-key, and thankfully, she has one. It's in a small metal key-box that's attached to the bottom of her porch swing.

I have to remember to talk to her about this key being out here. It's way too dangerous!

I unlock the door and slowly push the door open, but I don't step inside yet. I stay in the doorway. I can hear the TV on in the living room but that's the only noise I hear.

"Delaney?" I call out.

No answer.

"Delaney, are you home?"

Fuck it.

I take a deep breath, then walk in and close the door behind me. I kick off my shoes, then take off my coat and hang it up. I walk around the corner into the living room, and I get my answer as to why Delaney hasn't responded to my messages. She is passed the fuck out on the couch. One leg is hanging off the couch, and I'm actually surprised she hasn't fallen to the floor yet.

"Oh, Del. What the fuck have I done to you?"

I walk over to the couch and gently lift her leg back onto the couch, then pull the blanket off the back of the couch and lay it over her. I stand and stare down at the beautiful woman who has had my heart since I was a younger. I really fucked this up, and I have no idea if I'm ever going to be able to make it up to Delaney. I hope I can, but I just don't know. If I were her, I wouldn't forgive me, so I can't even be upset or mad if she never forgives me.

I grab the wine bottle off the table next to the couch and take it to the kitchen. Then I put the cap back on and put it in the fridge before I walk toward the fireplace. I pick up the picture of Delaney, Dylan, and me.

It was such a sad day. I still remember feeling completely devastated. I lost my best friend and the girl I had a major crush on all in the same day. And now I'm right back there. I've lost the woman I'm in love with, and chances are I'm going to lose my best friend once he finds out what I did—not that I would blame either of them.

I put the picture back, then sit on the couch opposite of where Delaney is. She is still out cold, and I'm sure she'll be fine, but I want to hang out for just a little bit and make sure. I pull my phone out and open Dylan's text thread. I know what I have to do. There's no avoiding it, and quite frankly, I need to man up and admit my shit.

I have to tell you something. Something I did. You're probably going to want to kick my ass.

Oh fuck. What did you do?

I opened this door, so there's no turning back now.

I came home to see Delaney. Only I didn't tell her who I was . . .

What are you talking about?

I approached her while she was on this really bad blind date. Told her my first name, but not last.

I really should just type everything out in one long message, then go back to the hotel, get my shit, and get the hell out of here before Dylan flies back and kills me. Though I do deserve it.

What the fuck are you getting at?

Fuck it.

I like your sister. More than like, actually. And I have for a long time. I'm not here on business; I came to see her. Only I chickened out and didn't tell her my last name. We hung out a couple of times and stuff happened. I kind of just fled and then she found out who I was and came to the hotel and ripped me a new ass.

What. Kind. Of. Stuff.

Here it comes . . .

We kissed a bit . . . and cuddled.

So my sister ripped you a new ass over kisses and cuddles? Bull.
Fucking. Shit. What else happened, Flynn?

I stand and pace around Delaney's living room.

Here goes nothing.

We almost had sex.

I wait for another message, but it doesn't come, and I imagine Dylan is planning how many ways he can kill me without getting caught right now. To be honest, I completely deserve it too. I know what I need to do, but it's going to be one of the hardest things I've ever done. But it's the only way. I walk toward the kitchen and find a notebook sitting on the kitchen island. I rip a piece of paper out, then grab a pen and sit down. I stare at the paper for a few moments and think about exactly what I want to say. I know what I need to say, but I'm finding it hard to even begin. I know that this is likely the end. And it sucks but I have no one to blame but myself. I take a deep breath, then finally start writing.

Delaney,

I am so sorry for what I did. Please believe me when I say that I never meant to hurt you. I've loved you for as long as I can remember, and I was afraid you wouldn't give me a chance if you knew who I was. I wanted you to get to know me as the man I am now, not the boy I was back then. I know that's no excuse, but I'm afraid that's all I've got. Excuses. I'm ashamed of myself, but I promise I'll leave you alone. I won't contact you again. You should know, I told your brother about what happened. I didn't do it to embarrass you; I did it because it was time for me to be a man and admit what I did. I hope you know I'll forever regret hurting you and breaking your trust. I wish things could be different, but I know it's too late for that. Again, I'm so sorry. Take care.

Always,

Flynn

I finish writing my letter, then fold it in half and write "Delaney" on the back, then leave it on the island. I walk back into the living room and check on Delaney again, who is still passed out and hasn't moved an inch. I crouch next to her and tuck a piece of hair behind her ear, then gently kiss her forehead before I stand back up. I stare at her for a few more seconds, then walk toward the front door. I put on my boots and coat and grab the spare key from the table near the door. I turn and look at Delaney again.

"Goodbye, my love," I say before I open the door and walk out of Delaney's house and out of her life.

Chapter 13

Delaney | Four Years Later

I can't believe I'm about to see the one person I never wanted to see again. It's been four years, and I've done the best I could to forget about him. It hasn't been easy, either. His excuses of why he did what he did actually made sense to me. I never said anything because he was Dylan's best friend and there was no way I would ever want to come between them. Plus, we were kids; I didn't even know what real love was. And then he showed up here and literally broke my heart. I get he was scared, but being scared does not excuse a total betrayal. I was so much more than betrayed; I was embarrassed. And for me, the embarrassment has been just as hard to get over as the betrayal. He kept his word, though; he didn't contact me again. I actually had no idea that he and Dylan were talking again until about two years after he left. Dylan told me he didn't speak to him for the longest time, but then they reconnected. I was upset at first—and rightfully so—but how could I selfishly tell my brother to never talk to his best friend again? And how could I shut my brother out of my life, just to stay away from Flynn? It wouldn't have been right. So I did my best to just forget about the past and forget about Flynn.

And for a long time, I did. But now we're being pushed back together because Dylan is moving home after being in Italy for the last few years, and he invited Flynn to his welcome home dinner. I wanted to stay home, but how could I? I haven't seen Dylan in years.

"Breathe, Del," Joy reminds me.

"I am. I think."

I've been panicked about this damn dinner ever since Dylan told me Flynn was coming. I knew they were talking again, but I didn't think Dylan was going to invite Flynn. I actually thought it was just going to be family, but then a few days ago, Dylan told me Flynn was, in fact, coming. After a pretty serious meltdown, I asked Joy if she could come, so I kind of had someone in my corner too. And thankfully, her and Jason didn't have any plans, so she more than happily agreed to come with me.

"Delaney, we can turn right around and leave if you want. I'm sure your brother would understand."

"Yes, he probably would understand, but my parents wouldn't. I haven't seen Dylan in years, and I should be there."

"Okay," Joy replies as we walk up the steps to my parents' house.

"Just promise me something?"

"Anything, Del."

"Please stay close, and if I look like I need to get the hell out of here, then please just get me out of here."

"Deal."

We stand on my parents' front porch for a few moments, and I close my eyes and take a few deep breaths before I open the door and walk into what I'm sure it's going to be a difficult night.

"There she is!"

I look to the left and don't even have time to take off my jacket before Dylan comes barreling toward me and pulls me into a big bear hug. I can't even hug back because my arms are pinned at my sides as my twin brother squeezes the hell out of me.

"Air . . . " I gasp.

"Dylan, let your sister go before you kill her," Mom says, walking up next to us.

Dylan finally lets go and I'm able to breathe again. I take a step back and look up at my twin brother. He looks good, but tired. When Mom called and told me Dad had asked him to come home to prepare to take over at the B&B, I was half insulted because they didn't ask me, and half super excited because I will finally get to see my brother on a regular basis again. Despite the fact that I was a little jealous that they asked him and not me, I wasn't sure if he would so willingly come home. I guess when it came down to it, it was no decision at all for him. He was happy to come home, and we were all super happy to see him.

"It's so good to see you, Dylan," I say, pulling him into a normal, not about to kill him, hug.

"It's good to see you too, sis. I've missed you."

"I've missed you too."

"Come everyone, let's get out of the foyer," Mom says. "I'll take your coats."

Joy and I both pull off our coats and scarves and hand them to Mom. She immediately goes upstairs, and I imagine she's laying them across the bed in what was my room. My room always seemed to be the coat closet whenever we had guests over. While I didn't mind it now, it was quite annoying back when I was growing up because I always had to fight a mountain of coats just to get to my bed.

"Where's Dad?" I ask, as Dylan, Joy, and I go into the living room and sit down.

"He ran to the store a little bit ago. Should be back any time now," Dylan replies.

Mom comes back downstairs and joins us. We're only sitting for a few minutes when I hear the front door swing open. Mom and Dylan share a look before they both quickly look away from one another.

"We're back!"

"*We're?*" I ask.

There's no time for a response, and I don't have to see him to know that he's here. He either went to the store with Dad or he just happened to be walking in as Dad came back. But he's here, and now I have to control myself as best I can. I look at Joy and she offers a small smile before she grabs my hand and squeezes gently.

I feel like I'm going to puke.

A few seconds later, Dad and Flynn walk into the living room. My arms break out in little goosebumps, and I feel like my heart is going to beat right out of my chest. I hate that he still has this effect on me. I should want to punch him in the mouth, not swoon at the sight of him. But he looks so fucking good.

Ugh, what is wrong with me?

"Hi, sweetheart!" Dad gushes.

"Hi, Daddy!" I reply, jumping up off the couch.

I rush toward him and throw my arms around him. He's standing so close to Flynn that I accidentally hit him as I hug Dad.

Serves you right. Jerk.

"How's my girl?"

"I'm good, Daddy. How have you been?" I reply before pulling away.

He keeps his arm around me, and I lay my head against his shoulder, completely ignoring Flynn. Joy looks at me, then covers her mouth as if she's hiding her smile.

"Not bad. Looking forward to taking a step back from the B&B."

"I bet," I reply.

I walk back over and sit on the couch next to Joy, and Dad goes and sits next to Mom. Flynn stands in the doorway, donning an awkward look, and I almost feel bad for him.

Almost.

"Are you gonna sit down?" Dylan asks Flynn.

"Uh . . . yeah. I have to go outside for a minute, though. I'll be back," Flynn replies before he turns and walks out the front door.

"Rude," I blurt out.

"Delaney," my brother snaps.

"What? Am I supposed to pretend that it's okay that he's here? I mean . . . I'm doing my best, but just seeing him again completely infuriates me."

Total lie. Seeing him again makes me feel something, but it's definitely not anger.

"What exactly happened that makes you so angry at Flynn, Delaney?" Mom asks.

"Nothing. I'm just not happy to see him. Not to mention the fact that I don't think he should be here. He isn't family."

"Neither is Joy," Dylan replies. "Sorry. No offense, Joy."

"None taken," Joy replies.

"Joy is more an extended family member than Flynn could ever be," I snap.

"You promised you would try, Del."

"I know I did. And I did. *I did try.* What more do you want from me? If you want, Joy and I will leave, and you can have dinner with Mom, Dad, and Flynn."

"You tried for, like, five minutes. You hit him when you went to hug Dad, and you didn't say a word to him. How is that *trying*?"

"You know what? I'm your sister, and he's the guy who showed up, lied about who he was, and humiliated me. How about you have my back and not his?"

I stand, storm out of the living room, and stomp my way upstairs to my old room. And for added dramatic effect, I slam the door shut. I realize I just partially told my parents what happened, but I'm not really sure that I give a shit. I plop down on my bed and my phone chimes in my pocket. I figure it's Joy telling me the escape car is ready to go. Instead, I see a name on my screen that I wasn't expecting.

I'm so sorry, Del. I shouldn't have come here.

My first thought is that I'm pissed off that he would use my nickname like we are best friends and he is apologizing for something simple. And my second thought is that I really don't want to reply because I'm not sure I trust what I'm going to say. He obviously kept my phone number, which makes me mad because I told him to lose it. But on the other hand, I kept his phone number when I swore to myself I was going to delete it.

I flop back onto my bed and stare at the ceiling. I remember being banished to my room when I was a kid, and Dylan and Flynn were having a boys-only sleepover in the living room. I would creep down the hallway and sit at the top of the stairs and listen to them talk about games and watch movies and joke around. I so badly wanted to be part of their group, but I was a girl and I didn't fit in. And then as I started to get a little bit older, I started to realize that I didn't have eyes for Flynn because I wanted to be a part of their boys' club but because I'd grown to have feelings for him. And then his family moved away, and my brother was pretty much devastated. I didn't have a choice but to hide my heartbreak because no one knew I had such a crush on Flynn. Everyone comforted Dylan because he literally lost his best friend, but me . . . ? I was never really that close to him, so no one would have understood why I was so upset when they left.

My phone chimes again, and I close my eyes and take a deep breath. Chances are it's another message from Flynn, and if I'm being completely honest, I'm not sure I have the strength to read another message and not respond. I figure I should at least see who it is, so I open my eyes and I'm about to check my phone when there's a knock at the door. I get up and cross my room, then pull the door open.

"Hey. Are you okay?" Joy asks.

"Not really. I thought I could do this. I thought I could see him again and pretend like nothing happened . . . but I can't."

"I know you love your brother, Delaney, but it was really quite shitty of him to ask you to do this. Especially since he knows what happened between you two."

I nod slightly, then wipe a tear away that started to fall down my cheek.

"I think I want to go."

"Then let's go. Your brother got up and went outside after you stormed off, and he hasn't come back yet. Your mom and I were talking, and I told her I thought we were probably going to leave. She wasn't upset or mad. It actually seemed like she understood."

"Okay. Let's do it. Get me out of here."

Chapter 14

Flynn

I knew I never should've agreed to come here tonight. I'm actually quite pissed off at Dylan because he told me he talked to Delaney about me coming and she was fine with it. But her reaction when I walked in the room clearly showed she was *not* okay with me being there. I stood outside on the porch after I walked out of the house. I heard Delaney and Dylan going back and forth a little bit, then I saw her storm past the door and up the stairs. I don't know why I thought it would be a good idea to send her a text message, but I did, and like I figured, she didn't respond. After that, I figured there was no point in me staying, so I got on my bike and took off.

Now I'm parked by the docks, just sitting here staring at the lake. It's late September, and it's chilly tonight, but not terrible. After I left four years ago, I decided to stay in New York State. I actually moved about an hour and a half away from here. I thought that maybe one day she would be able to forgive me, and I wanted to make sure that I was close enough to be able to get to her when that time came. Obviously, that time never came, and it probably won't ever come. She is still too hurt and angry over what I did, and she has every right. I can't be upset with that or argue it. I dug this hole I'm in and I seriously have no idea if I will ever get myself out of it.

My phone vibrates more than once in my pocket, so I pull it out and glance at it. There are two notifications from Dylan. I'd be lying if I said I'm not disappointed. I was hoping Delaney would message me, even if it was just to yell and curse at me. But I'm reminded once again that everything that happened is my fault, and as much as I want it, I don't deserve her forgiveness. I put my phone face-down on the dock beside me and stare off into the night. I don't even notice the headlights pull into the parking lot behind me or hear the footsteps walking down the dock toward me.

"Were you planning on just ignoring me?"

Great.

I should've known Dylan would know exactly where to look for me. He and I used to come here all the time and hang out and fish when we were younger. And then when my parents told me we would be moving, this is where I came to hide out. Dylan always knew to come here to find me if he couldn't find me at home.

"No. I just needed some time alone."

Dylan sits on the dock next to me. "You shouldn't have left."

"No, I shouldn't have come. We could've had our own dinner or drinks at the bar. I never should have agreed to come to your parents' house."

"Delaney was just being dramatic."

"I heard her yelling at you, you know. And she's right. She's your sister and you should have her back. I lied to her. I deceived her on purpose because I didn't want her to know who I was right away. You and I didn't talk for a long time after that, but you never kicked my ass for it, and I still don't know why."

"Dude, are you seriously asking me right now why I didn't kick the fuck out of you?"

"Yes! I am!" I yell.

"Look, what you did was seriously fucked up, and you definitely deserved to get your ass kicked by me, but I think the torture you're going through now—and have been for the last four years—is enough."

"What are you talking about?"

"I'm not stupid, Flynn. I knew you had a crush on my sister back when we were kids, and I knew she had a crush on you. Sure, I was upset when you moved, but Delaney was heartbroken, and I knew why. I figured if you guys found your way back to each other, then who was I to stand in the way?"

"But what I did was fucked up."

"Yeah, it was, but you're paying for it. The woman you love won't give you the time of day, and that has to be torture enough."

He's right. It is.

The day Delaney confronted me, she told me to lose her number and stay out of her life. I was able to do one of those things, but never the other. Over the years, I saw her number in my phone and wanted to reach out numerous times, but I never had the balls to actually do it. So for years, I just stared at her phone number in my phone. I tried to date and move on, but nothing ever felt right. I've known for a while that it's because if I were ever to settle down with a woman, it would've been with Delaney. But I'll never get that chance now, and that's something that I have to live with for the rest of my life.

"I don't think I can stay here, Dylan. I think I need to get the fuck out of here as soon as possible."

"I don't think you should run this time."

"What do you suggest I do, then?"

Dylan looks at me, and I can see an evil plan written all over his face. He is definitely up to something.

"I think you should stay here. You should come stay with me. Move in, actually. My condo has two bedrooms and two bathrooms, so you'll have your own space."

What is he playing at?

"Are you out of your fucking mind? Do you want your sister to never talk to you again?"

"If I know one thing about my sister, it's that she is always passionate when she cares."

"What are you saying?"

"Don't be a dumbass, dude. I'm saying she cares about you being back for more than one reason. Yes, she's probably still hurt because, let's face it, what you did really fucking sucked. But if she only hated you, she would completely ignore you."

"So the fact that she flipped out says . . . ?"

"It says that she isn't just angry; she still cares. A lot."

"I don't know, D," I reply in an unsure tone.

Sure, Dylan knows his sister better than anyone, but I'm not sure if he's right about this.

"I'm not saying it's going to be easy. You're probably gonna have to put up with a bunch of shit from her. But I don't think you should count yourself out just yet."

Dylan and me getting a place together sounds like a pretty awesome idea. We always talked about getting a place together and living life to the fullest—but that's when we were in our twenties. We're now in our mid-thirties, and I'm not sure what that says about two thirty-something-year-old men living together, but I have to admit it's a very tempting offer. To be honest, I would love nothing more than to prove to Delaney how sorry I am for what I did and prove to her that I am crazy about her, but realistically speaking, I'm not sure she would ever give me a chance again.

"What do you think?" Dylan asks.

What the hell. Carpe diem, right?

"Let's do it."

"Okay, good. Get your ass on your bike and let's go to the hotel and get your shit."

"You want to do this now?"

"Fuck yeah, dude. You have a lot of work to do if you want to win over my sister."

Dylan and I both stand and start walking down the dock toward the parking lot. I'm quite surprised that Dylan is so willing to help me, but at the same time I'm glad he is. I don't think I'd be able to get anywhere close to Delaney ever again by myself.

"So just out of curiosity, what the hell are you going to tell Delaney? I'm pretty sure she's going to be pissed when she finds out you let me move in with you."

"Oh, she's definitely going to be pissed, but like I said, I know my sister. I know she likes you as much as you like her. And to be honest dude . . . I think it would be cool as fuck if you and my sister got together."

"Why's that?" I ask as we approach our vehicles.

"Are you kidding? I always thought of you as a brother, and now you could be. We just have to get you there."

He's definitely right there. When we were growing up, we always referred to one another as brother, and I think it would be really awesome to say that Dylan was, in fact, my brother. Brother-in-law, but still, a brother.

Dylan gets in his car and I hop on my bike, and a few minutes later, we leave and head toward the hotel. Once there, it doesn't take long to get my shit packed up and into Dylan's car. I didn't actually bring much because I was expecting this to be a very long trip.

"We should go to your place and get more of your shit," Dylan says before we leave the hotel.

"Nah, it's okay. I'll just go shopping over the next few days."

Money really isn't an issue for me, so I won't have any problems paying for my place there until my lease is up, as well as chipping in here. But

I do have to make sure I call my boss tomorrow and let him know I'm resigning from my position.

"I know you said your parents left you with a pretty good cushion, but if you're looking for work, you're more than welcome to come join me at the B&B."

"Do you really think it would be a good idea for me to work at the B&B where Delaney also works?"

"No, it would probably be a terrible idea, but it would show Delaney that you're trying."

Damn, he's good.

"Fair enough," I reply before I kickstart my bike to life.

Dylan gets in the car, then pulls out of the parking lot and I follow closely behind. I'm not sure if this plan is going to work, but I'm willing to give it a shot. Delaney is absolutely worth me giving it my all, and I will keep doing so for as long as it takes.

Chapter 15

Delaney

I wake up the next morning with an absolute pounding in my head. I'm not sure what the hell time Joy and I finally passed out, but I know we drank a lot of wine. When we got here, I didn't actually plan on getting wasted, but the more I thought about seeing Flynn again, the more glasses of wine I poured. At one point, I remember Joy having to take my phone away from me because I was dangerously close to calling Flynn.

I lay here, feeling like shit, for at least twenty minutes before I'm finally able to pull my ass out of bed. As soon as I stand, the headache gets worse and I want nothing more than to crawl back into bed and pull the blankets up over my head, but I know I need to get my ass moving. I slink my way into my bathroom and quickly pee, then wash my hands and take some ibuprofen and drink a glass of water. Afterward, I make my way downstairs and go right to the kitchen to start a pot of coffee. My cell phone is sitting on the kitchen island, and I'm guessing that's where Joy left it when she left this morning. I vaguely remember her telling me she was going to spend the night, but that she had to leave before ten because she has to work today. Thankfully, I don't have to worry about that because I'm off for a few days.

Once the coffee is going, I grab my phone and walk into the living room and plop down on the couch. I unlock my screen and see I have a message from my brother, a message from Joy, and a message from Mom.

Hi, hon. Just wanted to check on you and see if you're okay. Your
father and I will be at the B&B today if you want to stop by and
have breakfast. Love you.

Fat chance of that happening, considering it's already after eleven and
I feel like death warmed over.

Hey, Del. Just wanted to check in see how you're feeling today.
We sure did drink a LOT of wine last night. I have no idea how
I managed to wake up this morning, but I feel like hell. Text me
later. xoxo

It's good to know I'm not the only one who feels like ass right now.

I stare at my phone for a few seconds, and I'm not sure whether or
not I want to open up Dylan's message. I love my brother—he is my
twin—but I'm not sure if I can be okay with him if he is going to side
with Flynn. I think about it for a few more seconds, then decide to hold
off on checking Dylan's message right now. I put my phone on the coffee
table while I go into the kitchen and make a huge cup of coffee. Like my
wineglasses, all of my coffee cups are oversized, and I wouldn't have it any
other way.

A couple of minutes later, I'm parked back on the couch with the TV
on and my coffee cup in my hand. My cell phone is sitting next to me
on the armrest, and I'm still on the fence about reading my brother's
message. I drink my coffee and continuously flip through TV channels,
but nothing grabs me. I don't really have any plans for today, but I heard
it's supposed to be a pretty decent day, so I'm thinking about getting
dressed and walking the town a little bit. A little walking and thinking
will probably be good for me.

In all honesty, I need to figure out what I'm going to do about Flynn.
My brother coming home means that not only will we get to see him
more but also Flynn will probably be here more and I'm going to run
into him from time to time. I don't want to stay so hostile toward him,
but I have to try to hide behind hostility. If I let my guard down for even

the smallest amount of time, I'm afraid he'll work his way back into my heart. And I feel like it'll end in heartbreak once again. I'm not sure that I could survive losing him a second time.

I take a big gulp of coffee, then put my cup down on the table and grab my phone. I feel like I might need a little perspective here, and I know Joy will give it to me.

Morning. First of all, thank you for staying last night. I really needed a girls' night. And second, THANK YOU for taking my phone from me. The last thing I needed was a list of drunk texts to Flynn. So, thank you, thank you, thank you!

I don't remember exactly what time Joy said she had to work today, but I'm sure she's either on her way or she will be soon enough, so I'm not surprised when her response comes a few seconds later.

Of course! You know I'll always have your back. How are you feeling?

Tbh? Like shit. About everything. I need some advice. When you have time.

I have time now. What's up?

Here we go.

I need your God's honest opinion about everything. Am I over-reacting when it comes to Flynn? I mean, I know what he did four years ago was shitty and terrible, but it's been four years. Should I let it go? Am I being ridiculous?

I've never been one to hold a grudge for long, and I'm really starting to wonder if it's even worth it to still be so angry about everything. Was it fucked up? Yes, of course! But he apologized, multiple times. And he even walked away and stayed out of my life. I also have to look at the fact that my brother is friends with him again. He didn't kill him like I thought he would've. So maybe I'm just being overly dramatic about everything.

As a woman, I think you have every right to still be upset with him for what he did. As a person, I think you are holding onto your anger because it's a lot easier to hide the fact that you still have feelings for him when you're angry and hostile.

Nailed it.

I'll be honest, I don't know what to do. I have not seen that man in four years, but the moment he walked into the room last night, I felt everything come rushing back to the surface. I don't know how to make it stop.

Maybe you shouldn't make it stop? Maybe you should embrace it and see where it takes you?

I'm scared.

True. Freaking. Story.

I know you are. Love can be scary. But you're never going to know unless you drop the wounded-woman act and give him a chance.

I asked for her honest opinion, but now that I have it, I'm not sure I want it. I'm not sure I can just turn off the hurt he caused when he lied to me. That betrayal hurt me more than anything has ever hurt me in my entire life.

How do I get past the betrayal, though?

Take it one step at a time. Day by day. Don't jump in headfirst. Go extremely slow until you know what his intentions are. I'm not sure what's going to happen, but I'll be honest—he could have slept with you that night at your place, but he didn't. Something stopped him. In my honest opinion, I think he likes you just as much as you like him and you're both struggling with it.

I guess I could send him a message and see what happens.

Exactly. You won't know unless you try.

Okay. I'll give it a go. Thanks, Joy. You're the best! xoxo

I put my phone on the end table next to the couch and grab my coffee cup and take a long drink. Then I put my cup down and snuggle down with my blanket. My head is pounding less than before, but I still have a headache and I could probably use some more sleep. If I'm going to extend an olive branch to Flynn, then I have to be one hundred percent in my right mind. And right now, I'm not, because I'm so fucking hungover.

I lay there and stare about the ceiling, and I can't help but wonder about what's to come. I'm not sure where Flynn went last night. I'm not sure if he's still in town, or if he left. But I do know that if I'm going to extend an olive branch, so to speak, then I'm going to have to send him a message and see if he wants to meet up. I don't think it's wise to have him come here, so maybe we can meet at the coffee shop. Take it back to where he and I first saw each other again.

I close my eyes and try to get some more sleep, but my mind is moving like crazy and I can't seem to calm down enough to actually fall asleep. I grab my phone off the table and open up my brother's message.

Hey sis. I'm sorry that last night went the way it did. I'll always have your back, you know that, but I think this situation is more complicated than just me having your back. I think there's something between you and Flynn, and it's up to the two of you to decide what to do with that.

Holy shit.

You know?

Of course I do. You're my twin. I know you better than anyone. I don't know what you want to do, but I will tell you this . . . Flynn is moving in with me and I offered him a position at the B&B.

Oh, my god.

Why?!

I told you—because I think there's something between you two and it's unfinished. Only the two of you can decide what to do with it, Delaney, but please don't let your stubbornness ruin something that might turn out to be pretty awesome.

Well, shit.

Who are you, and what have you done with my brother?

Ha ha. Funny. Funny.

I stare at my phone. I'm not sure what to say. I never expected Dylan to be okay with the idea of Flynn and I dating, nor did I expect him to actually try to push us together. And then there's the fact that Flynn is moving in with Dylan, which means he's going to be around a lot more. That's potentially problematic in itself. What happens if we do try to date, and we just can't make it work? Then it's awkward for everyone. I know I shouldn't be thinking this far ahead, but I can't help it. My mind is literally ping-ponging back and forth right now. I guess I should start by sending Flynn a message, then go from there. I take a deep breath, then pull up his number.

I can do this. It's going to be fine.

Hi.

I definitely planned to say more, but I'm not even sure if he's going to answer, so I think it's best to just open the line of communication and see if he responds.

Hi. Is everything okay?

Here we go.

Yes. Why wouldn't it be?

I guess I'm just surprised that you're messaging me. I'm glad you are, but I have to ask. Why are you?

Oh, you know . . . my best friend and my brother both talked some sense into me.

I think we should talk.

Okay. I'm free whenever you are.

I'm a bit hungover right now, but maybe later?

Sounds great. Hungover, huh? Need me to bring you anything?

Tempting. Having Flynn come here would be so much easier, but I'm really not sure if it's a good idea. I want us to be able to talk in a neutral place where we won't be tempted to do anything. Especially if he's still feeling anything remotely close to what I'm feeling. I mean, it's been years since he and I have seen each other besides last night, and he might have moved on. That's something I'm going to have to live with.

I think I'm good for now. Going to try to take a nap, I think. Maybe we can meet in town for coffee either later today or tomorrow?

It's a date. Not a date-date, but we'll be meeting, so it'll be like a date. A friend date. Yes. Friend date.

He's rambling. How cute. Maybe he does still like me.

I'll text you later, Flynn.

Okay. Later, Del.

Once again, I put my phone down on the table and stare up at the ceiling. For the first time in years, I am not angry when I think about Flynn or think about seeing him. It's entirely possible I was holding onto my anger so I didn't have to face the other feelings, but now that those other feelings are out in the open and apparent to other people, I'm ready to let go of the anger.

I'm starting to think there's a pretty good chance that everything could work out, and I have to say I'm really looking forward to it. Flynn and I had so much chemistry and passion between us when he came here four years ago, and I can only hope it'll be the same, if not stronger, now. I can't wait to feel his hands on my body again. To feel his lips on mine again. To have his body pressed up against mine. I know we need to try to take things slowly and talk through everything, but I can't help but feel excited and look forward to the future now.

We were both worried about how Dylan would take us being together, which is why I never told him how I felt back when we were kids and why he didn't tell me his last name when he came here for years ago. But

Dylan has given us his blessing. He told me that the ball is basically in my court, and it's up to me to figure out what to do with it. So I'm giving it a go.

Chapter 16

Delaney

I wake up a little later and the very first thing I realize is that my head is no longer pounding.

Thank God.

I grab my phone off the table and check the time. It's already after one o'clock, so I hop off the couch. I check my phone as I head toward my bathroom, and I have a message from Flynn and one from my brother. I can't help but smile when I see Flynn's name. It almost feels as if I woke up a completely different person. Like all of my anger vanished while I was sleeping and now I'm looking at everything in a new light.

Hey, sis. Flynn canceled on me for this afternoon. Thanks a lot! *crying face* JK. Have fun but be good!

I can't help but roll my eyes. My brother is such a butthead, but I have no idea what I would do without him. I close his thread and open Flynn's next.

Hey, Del, just wanted to check on you and see how you're doing. Text me later.

Hey. I'm awake. I'm much better. Thank you for asking. I was able to get more sleep, and I just woke up a few minutes ago . . . headache free. Thank goodness.

Good deal.

Text bubbles appear, then disappear, and reappear then disappear, and no other message comes. I'm kind of thinking something might be up, but he's afraid to say it or ask it.

Are you okay?

While I wait for a response, I walk into my closet and pick out some clothes for today. I'm thinking a hoodie, jeans, and boots will suffice, so I get everything out and lay it on my bed. Then, I walk into the bathroom to start the shower. It's not super cold outside yet, but I still like to let the bathroom warm up before I get in, so Flynn has another five minutes to answer before I won't be able to respond for at least a half hour. I wait and wait, but he doesn't message me back, so I start to take off my clothes. I'm about to step into the shower when my phone chimes on the counter. I wrapped my towel around myself and quickly rush over to grab my phone.

Yes, I'm fine. I just wanted to make sure we're still good for today? Coffee in town?

Ah. He thought I was going to change my mind.

I didn't change my mind, Flynn. I'll see you in about an hour. *winky face*

After last night, I'm sure he's probably nervous about seeing me face-to-face. For all I know, he might think I'm planning to meet up with him and then scream at him in public or something crazy like that. But I really did wake up feeling completely different about everything. We were both wrong four years ago. He was wrong because he didn't tell me his last name, but I was also wrong because I never even asked. As a woman living alone—even though this is a small town where everyone knows everyone—I should've known better.

I put my phone back on the counter, then hang my towel up and get in the shower. I've always been a long shower taker. I was never one to just wash my hair, wash my body, and be done. I love relaxing under the water. I take my time washing my hair. Today is a condition day, so I take time doing that as well. Then I wash my body until I'm a big, lathered-up, soapy sud and shave my legs, because why not? After I rinse off, I rinse out my hair, then stand under the spray for a bit longer. Today could be the start of something new and exciting. You can't fake the kind of chemistry we had, and I'm honestly really hoping it works out.

By the time I finally get out of the shower, my hands are wrinkly, but I feel more relaxed than I have in a while. I quickly wipe off the mirror, then pull a brush through my hair. I grab my dryer and get my hair dried and styled relatively quickly, then I brush my teeth and walk into my bedroom. Not even ten minutes later, I'm dressed and ready to go. I've never gotten showered and dressed so quickly, but I'm excited to get this 'friend date' underway.

I rush down the hallway and grab my jacket, slip my phone into my pocket, and grab my keys off the table. I'm about to walk out the door when I realize I never actually texted Flynn to tell him what time we were meeting. I only said that I would see him in about an hour. So I pull my phone back out of my pocket and open his text thread.

Hey. What time were you thinking about heading to the coffee shop?

I can be there whenever you need me to be there. Why, what's wrong?

Nothing's wrong. I'm ready to walk out the door right now, so I was thinking we could meet up now.

Sounds good.

Okay, good. I'll see you in a few minutes.

I slip my phone back into my pocket, put on my coat, and head out. It's really not too bad out today, which I'm loving. The closer I get to the coffee shop, the more nervous I seem to get. By the time I'm standing at the coffee shop's front door, I've almost completely talked myself out of this. I look in through the door, and I don't see Flynn. I take a couple of steps backward and I'm about to turn around and go back home when I bump into a wall.

"Are you okay?"

I don't even have to turn around to know whose voice it is. A shiver passes through me, and I take a deep breath before I turn around and stand face-to-face with Flynn.

My god.

I attempt to form words but I'm having trouble doing so. If it's at all possible, Flynn seems to look even sexier now than he did last night.

"Delaney? You okay?"

Speak, idiot!

I clear my throat, then nod my head. "Yes. I'm fine."

"Okay. Are you ready to go in?"

"Yes. And sorry I bumped into you."

"It's okay. Though I'm wondering where you were going. Were you changing your mind?"

Don't lie.

"Honestly? I was definitely thinking about running."

"Why? I thought you wanted to meet up?"

"I did. I *do.* Come on. Let's go inside," I reply, walking toward the door.

"Are you sure?" Flynn asks, coming up behind me.

"Yes."

I pull the door to the coffee shop open and walk in, and Flynn follows closely behind me. There's no line right now, so we're able to go right up to the counter. A few minutes later, we both have our coffees in our hands and we're standing awkwardly near the counter.

"So, what now?" Flynn asks, his eyebrows lifted.

"This is pretty awkward. I'm sorry . . . "

"The weather isn't too bad today. Do you want to go for a walk now that we have our coffees?"

"Yes. Let's do that," I reply.

Flynn leads the way, and I follow him out of the coffee shop. He heads in the direction of the lake and I'm kind of glad he does. I love everything about our small town, but I especially love the lake. There's something so serene about it, and it always seems to calm me whenever I am having a moment.

"I'm really glad you wanted to meet up today, Delaney," Flynn says as we walk toward the lake.

"I'll be honest. I wasn't sure about it. But then Dylan and my best friend, Joy, both talked some sense into me, and I decided it would probably be a good idea."

"Why weren't you sure?"

"Because it's not like we had a good ending the last time we saw each other."

"I know. And I'm so sorry about that," Flynn replies sadly.

"I know you are. It wasn't just your fault, you know."

"What do you mean?"

"I should have asked you your last name. I never did. It never even crossed my mind to ask you."

"I should have just told you, though."

"Yes, you should have, but I should have asked you too. I just felt so attracted to you and you were so familiar to me, and I just went with that."

We reach the lake, but we stop walking before we step out onto the dock.

"Do you want to sit?" Flynn asks me.

"Sure." I nod.

Flynn leads the way as we walk down the dock toward the bench that's at the end. It's really quite a lovely day, despite being just a little chilly. Once we reach the bench, we both sit. Awkward silence takes over while we drink our coffees, and I kind of forget why I wanted to meet up in the first place. Plus, Flynn is giving off a weird vibe, so I'm not sure what to do or say now.

"Nice day," Flynn says, breaking the silence.

"Yes. It's nice out," I agree.

"Why does this feel so awkward?" Flynn asks.

I'm glad he said it because this definitely feels awkward. My guess is the stuff that happened in the past is making it awkward now since we don't really know where to go from here. And if I'm being completely honest, I literally have no idea where we go from here. I want to put what happened way in the past. I want to trust Flynn and get to know him as an adult, but I can't calm that little voice inside of my head. The one that is telling me to proceed with extreme caution.

"I have a theory . . . "

"What's that?" Flynn asks.

"Completely honest answer?"

"Yes."

"I'm nervous you're going to lie to me about something again. And I think you're nervous because you think I'm going to start screaming again. Or something close to that."

Flynn doesn't say anything right away, and I think I either hit the nail on the head or I'm completely wrong. Maybe I shouldn't have said anything . . .

"I'm really afraid you aren't going to be able to forgive me," Flynn finally admits.

Time to go balls to the walls, Delaney!

"This probably isn't going to be easy, Flynn. But I want to try if you do. I liked you so much when we were kids, but you were my brother's best friend. I was worried about how you would take it, and how Dylan would. So I never said anything. Then you came back into my life, and even though I didn't know who you were, we clicked so fast and had such chemistry. I want to try if you do. I just need you to promise that you'll be truthful with me from here on out."

Flynn doesn't say anything for a few seconds, but he quickly takes my hand in his and gives it a light squeeze before he turns to face me.

"I've been crazy about you for such a long time, Delaney. And I'm so incredibly sorry I was such an idiot four years ago. I don't deserve it, but I would love nothing more than to get a second chance. I promise I'll never lie to you about anything ever again."

This is it. We're really going to do this.

"Okay. I promise I will do my best not to bring up the past again. And I will focus on getting to know *this* you, not the four-years-ago you."

"And I promise I will be the very best version of myself from here on out."

"Okay," I reply with a smile. "So . . . now what?"

"Well, you said you want to get to know me, so let's talk. What do you want to know?"

I want to know everything.

"What do you do for work now?" I ask.

I'm not sure why that's the first thing that comes to mind, but it does, so I ask it.

"Well . . . I resigned from my position to move here. My parents set me up with a pretty hefty fund before they retired to Florida, so I'm fine not working right now. But your brother did tell me I could come to the B&B for a job if I wanted to."

"Of course he did," I reply with a little more sass than I mean to. "Sorry."

"It's okay. What about you? Are you staying at the B&B now that your brother is going to be taking over?"

"I'm not really sure. I always thought Dad would put me in charge since I've been managing it for years now. I was pretty salty when he told me Dylan was coming home to take over as the lead innkeeper."

"I get it. You work hard; you deserve to be in charge as much as Dylan does. Why can't you both run it? Be co-innkeepers."

"It's not a terrible idea. I think Dylan and I would work well together."

"Of course, you would. You're twins.

"I guess . . . " I take a sip of my coffee before I look at him again. "I have another question."

Flynn nods. "Go ahead."

"Where have you been the last four years?"

"I lived about an hour from here, in Pleasant Valley. I wished every single day that you find it in your heart to forgive me and maybe give me another chance. I didn't want to be too far from you, just in case that day came."

Oh my goodness.

"I never stopped thinking about you, ya know," I admit quietly.

"I never stopped thinking about you either, Del. Not for a second." Flynn smiles at me and I swear my heart skips a beat.

"Can I ask you something?"

"Shoot," I reply.

"Did you ever try to move on?"

Tell the truth, Delaney.

"I did." I stare down at my shoes. "I dated a little. But no one ever came close. How about you?"

"I dated. But it never seemed right, so I stopped trying."

No one says anything for a little bit as we both just stare out at the lake. It's so peaceful and calm. A beautiful fall day. A perfect day, actually. Perfect weather, and perfect company.

"So . . . " I begin.

"Yes?"

"I'm not really sure what to talk about to be honest," I reply with a chuckle.

"I'm not either. I know I want to spend time with you; I'm just not sure what to talk about."

"You're not alone in that, Flynn. I'm not sure what to talk about, either."

"So, what do you want to do?"

"I'm not sure," I reply honestly. "What do you want to do?"

"I have an idea. But I'm not sure if you'll want to do it."

"What is it?" I ask.

"I was thinking maybe we could go back to your house and have a movie date?"

"A *date*, huh?"

I'm a little nervous about Flynn coming back to my place but putting our attention on a movie might be a good thing. It'll definitely take some of the awkwardness out of this if our attention is on something other than one another.

"Yes. Definitely. What do you say?"

This is it; this is the beginning of what could be a relationship between Flynn and I. Unlike last time, I definitely want to take things slow, especially until we get to know one another better. But I also can't deny how badly I want to kiss him right now. The chemistry we shared four years ago definitely has not gone anywhere. It's still here . . . and it is very strong.

"Let's do it." I stand.

Flynn stands and grabs his coffee cup off the bench with his left hand. Then, with his right hand, he intertwines his fingers with mine. My heart is absolutely pounding, and I feel nervous and warm all over, though I do my best to try to hide it. Flynn looks at me and smiles as we begin to walk to my house, and to our first official date.

Chapter 17

Flynn

My heart is pounding in my chest the entire walk back to Delaney's house. Every day that I was gone, I'd hoped I would get another chance with her. After a while, I figured that chance would never come—mostly because I didn't deserve it. Then, Dylan got in touch with me, and we slowly became friends again. It felt amazing to have my best friend back, but I just couldn't get Delaney out of my mind or my heart. And I really tried. But she was just too hard to forget about.

About a year after we started talking again, Dylan told me that he was moving back home and was going to take over at the B&B. I was excited that my best friend would be living here again. Maybe it would give me the opportunity I needed to try to get back in Delaney's good graces. And that's exactly what happened.

So far, this seems to be heading in the right direction and I couldn't be happier. I just have to make sure I don't fuck it up. I meant what I said—I won't lie to her again about anything. From now on, Delaney is getting the whole truth and nothing but the truth, no matter the situation.

"Are you going to come in?"

It takes me a few seconds to realize we're already at Delaney's house and she is standing in the doorway looking at me. I don't know how I managed to miss the fact that we were already here, but I definitely did.

"Yes. Sorry," I say, then smile.

Delaney narrows her eyes before she steps aside and allows me to walk into her house. The first thing I notice when I walk into the house is that Delaney has it completely decorated for Halloween. Purple lights are hung all over the place, and she has pumpkins and leaf garland everywhere as well. The second thing I notice is that Delaney has done a bit of work in here. Her once plain-colored walls are now painted red, and she has a new black sectional.

"The place looks good, Del."

"Thanks. It needed sprucing up, so I painted, got some new furniture, and a bigger TV," she replies proudly.

"I like it."

Delaney smiles as she pulls her jacket off and hangs it on the coatrack. Then she kicks her shoes off and walks into the living room. I do the same with my coat and shoes, then follow her. Delaney sits in the recliner opposite the couch, and I instantly recognize it as the recliner that used to sit in the spare bedroom. I sit on the couch, and I can't help but feel slightly uncomfortable. Either she doesn't trust me enough to sit near me or I am completely misreading the situation.

"I thought of another question," Delaney blurts out.

"I'm an open book. Ask away."

"Why did you come here, leave me a note, then leave?"

Shit.

I never for a moment considered that Delaney would ask me about that. To be honest, I kind of figured she'd forgotten about it or something.

Truth only.

"You were drunk texting me, and then you stopped answering. I was really worried about you. Was trying to figure out what to do. I couldn't text Dylan because he was in Italy, and what could he do? I didn't have any your best friend's number or your parents, so I decided to come and just make sure you were okay."

"How'd you get in?"

"I searched around outside until I found your hide-a-key," I reply honestly.

"I don't remember you coming here."

"No, you wouldn't. You were passed out on the couch. Hanging half off it, actually."

"That's embarrassing. What else happened?"

"Nothing. I watched you for a little bit, then cleaned up a little. While sitting here, I decided it was time to man up and text Dylan about what I did."

"That's when you told him?"

"Yes. I had to. Afterward, I wrote you that letter, and then walked out of your life."

"I don't remember much of that day, but I remember waking up and making a beeline for the bathroom. After throwing up for God knows how long, I made my way to the kitchen where I found your note. I was . . . devastated all over again."

"I'm sorry," I reply sadly.

"It's okay.

"No, it isn't. I was trying to do the right thing. What you demanded. But I only hurt you more."

"Look . . . I was crushed, but you did what I told you to. And to be honest, I was so angry back then that I really don't think I would have been able to see past my anger if you had stayed."

She's probably right. At the time, leaving was the best option. It hurt like hell, but it was the right thing to do given what I let happen. Plus, I'm not sure if we would be here right now if I hadn't left four years ago. I think the time and space did us both good, and now we're able to look at each other with new eyes.

"What movie do you want to watch?" Delaney asks, pulling me from my thoughts.

"Whatever you want to watch. I'm giving you complete control."

"So, if I say some girly chick-flick, you'll be fine with it?"

"Yes," I reply honestly.

And I will. I just want to spend time with her again. I'm willing to watch or do pretty much anything.

"Do you want more coffee?"

I forgot how much Delaney loves her coffee.

"I'd love some more." I nod.

Delaney smiles, then grabs the remote off the table next to her recliner and tosses it at me.

"Here . . . you pick a movie. I'm going to make popcorn and coffee," she says, getting up.

"Okay, sounds good."

Delaney is only in the kitchen for a minute or two when my phone starts vibrating in my pocket. I pull it out and see messages from Dylan.

Hey there, stud. How's it going? *winky face*

Asshole.

Fuck off.

LOL! I'm just kidding. But for real . . . how's it going?

It's going fine so far.

What are you guys doing?

We went for coffee and took a walk near the lake. Now we're at her house, about to watch a movie.

My sister hasn't killed you yet, so that's a good sign. Keep up the good work. *winky face*

What a shithead.

I'm focused on my phone, and I don't hear Delaney walk up behind the couch.

"Here's the popcorn," Delaney says, handing me the popcorn.

I jump slightly, but then shift my body so it looks like I was just getting comfortable. Delaney giggles behind me so I know she knows she scared me.

"Oh, uh . . . thanks."

"So did he message you too?"

"I don't know what you're talking about," I lie jokingly.

"You are so full of crap, it's pathetic."

"Yes, I am. He asked me how it was going. I don't remember him always being this damn nosy."

"Oh, he always was. And it got worse as he got older," she replies with a chuckle.

Delaney walks around the couch, then sits one cushion away from me. I put the popcorn bowl in between us, and Delaney looks at me and smiles.

"So, what are we watching?"

I have no goddamn idea how I'm going to sit here and focus on a movie. I'm thinking I should probably put on some kind of action movie or maybe horror. Anything with sex in it or romance is most likely going to get me in trouble. I know Delaney said she wants to take this slow, and I am completely okay with that, but I can't seem to calm the horny man inside me. The man who can smell the faint scent of her perfume. The man who wants nothing more than to grab her, pull her into my lap, and kiss the fuck out of her.

"*Hello*? Earth to Flynn."

"What? Did you say something?"

"Yes, I asked you what movie we're watching."

"Sorry. Umm, I'm not sure. What are you in the mood for?"

"Are you okay, Flynn?"

"Yeah. Why?" I reply.

"You're acting kind of funky."

Oh, I'm fine. I just can't stop thinking about kissing you.

"I have to use your bathroom," I say, abruptly standing.

"Okay. Down the—"

"Hall, first door on my right. I remember. Thanks."

I walk down the hall and go into the bathroom, then shut the door behind me. I need a minute to myself. It's becoming abundantly clear that I should've just taken her for coffee and then we should've gone our separate ways for today. I never should've come back to her house. Hell, I never should've suggested it. For the last four years, all I've been able to think about—even when I was trying to move on—was Delaney. How her lips felt when they were pressed up against mine. How her body felt when my hands were wandering.

I turn on the sink and splash some water on my face, then stare at my reflection in the mirror.

"Get it together," I mutter.

I lean down and splash some more water on my face, then turn the faucet off when there is a soft knock at the door.

"Flynn? Are you okay?"

Fuck, why is this so hard?

I quickly dry off my hands and face, then toss the towel into the hamper before I pull the bathroom door open.

"Hey. Yeah, I'm fine," I reply, stepping into the hallway.

Delaney doesn't look like she's buying it, but she doesn't say anything. She turns and walks back down the hall into the living room, and I follow closely behind her. We both sit back on the same couch with the popcorn bowl in between us, and I pick up the remote from the end table and turn on the TV.

"So, what are you thinking?" I ask.

Delaney grabs the remote out of my hand, clicks a few buttons, and the next thing I know, a movie is playing.

"Are you serious right now?" I ask, amused.

"What?" Delaney asks innocently.

"You're the girl who damn near jumped into my lap the last time we watched a scary movie together. You just put on a classic Stephen King horror movie. Are you for real right now?"

"I may have developed a knack for scary movies over the last few years. And I totally blame you."

"I'm so proud," I reply with a huge, shit-eating grin.

"Yeah, yeah. Shut up and watch the movie."

Delaney looks at me, and I can tell she's joking around because she's wearing a huge grin. Truth be told, I am quite proud of her. I never would've guessed she would willingly watch horror movies, considering that the last time we watched a scary movie together, she was an absolute chickenshit. But here she is, picking a classic Stephen King horror movie. I swear, I could marry this girl.

Chapter 18

Delaney

I knew Flynn was struggling. I could tell the moment we sat down in the living room. He doesn't hide his discomfort very well. I actually thought he was going to leave when he stood, but he went to the bathroom instead. But when he didn't come out, I was worried he climbed out the window or something. I knew I needed to do something, and quick. I was uncomfortable. Flynn was uncomfortable. And the last thing I wanted was for him to go home. Despite everything, I really do love that we are able to spend time together again. So soon as we got back into the living room, I decided to grab the remote out of his hand and take control of the situation. I knew Flynn was going to give me shit the moment I clicked on the movie. I honestly don't think I would've survived watching a movie with any kind of romance, kissing, or sex in it.

I remembered Dylan had once told me that Flynn was a huge Stephen King fan, so it was a no-brainer what movie I was going to put on.

"I can't freaking believe that you just turned on *Storm of the Century*. Have you seen it before?"

"No, but I remember you are a Stephen King fan, so I'll give it a go," I reply.

In the last few years, I'd become more accepting of the idea of watching scary movies, but deep down, I'm still a massive chickenshit. I'm sure Flynn will end up making fun of me at some point.

"You're awesome."

"Thanks. I'm glad you've already realized it."

"I've always known it, Delaney."

Oh my . . .

"So, we have popcorn, we have our movie, do you want anything to drink before I hit play?"

"Nope. I'm all set for right now. Let's get this show on the road."

"Sounds good," I reply, hitting play.

Something I don't mention is that I've seen this movie before, so I know when the semi-scary parts happen. Joy and I decided to have a Halloween movie night last year, and we decided to watch movies that were based off Stephen King novels. I'd be lying if I said I wasn't thinking about Flynn the whole time we were watching the movies though, because I knew that he was a huge fan. But also because it was me, Joy, and Jason. I definitely felt like a third wheel, but I sucked it up and ignored the pain in my heart. The pain that told me that, no matter how much I tried, I was missing Flynn terribly.

"Can I ask you something?"

"Sure. What's up?" I reply.

"Should you move over so I can protect you?"

Shithead.

I should say no so I can keep a cushion in between us, but I would be lying if I said I didn't want to feel that closeness with him again. I pick up the popcorn bowl and set it in Flynn's lap before I scooch over. There's a thin gap between our bodies, and I'm immediately aware of the fact that there is a LOT of sexual tension in this room. I know I said I wanted to take things slow, but realistically speaking, I'm not sure I can even adhere to my own request. I was worried at first that maybe the time would've changed how I felt about Flynn and how he felt about me, but it's abundantly clear the distance only made us want each other that much more.

I do my best to pay attention to the movie and I'm pretty sure Flynn is doing the same, but there are a few times where I feel like I'm going to lose it. And each and every one of those times occus because our hands are both in the popcorn bowl and we touch. After the third time our hands touch, I decide to forget about the popcorn altogether and just focus on the movie. Thankfully, that method works, and we make it through the first half of the movie.

"Do you want something to drink now?" I ask.

I already know what he's going to ask for if he asks for a drink, and thankfully, I happen to have it.

"I could really go for a beer right now. Do you have any?"

Nailed it.

"Actually, I do. I made sure to get some as soon as I heard Dylan was coming home."

I get up off the couch and make my way into the kitchen. I grab two beers from the fridge, then pop the tops off before I walk back into the living room. I sit back down on the couch and hand Flynn his beer. I made sure to leave a little bit more space between us this time, but I'm hoping Flynn doesn't really notice. I take a long swig, then put my bottle on the end table.

"So, are we ready for the second half of the movie?" I ask.

"Absolutely," Flynn replies with a nod.

"Okay then, let's do this."

We get through half of the second part of the movie when my phone starts chiming away. It has to be my brother again—nobody else would be this annoying. I pause the movie, then stand up.

"Sorry. Give me a second," I say.

"No problem."

I walk over to the kitchen and grab my phone off the island. There are three notifications from Dylan, and I can't help but roll my eyes when I see his name. He knows Flynn is at my house right now, and he's definitely doing his best to be an annoying pain in the ass.

Hi sis!

How's it going? *wink wink*

Okay, the reason I'm bugging you is because I wanted to see if you will still be able to pick up the pumpkins for the B&B today?

Shit. I totally forgot.

"Crap."

"What's wrong?"

"I forgot I was supposed to pick up pumpkins for the B&B today."

"Let's do it!" Flynn says, suddenly standing up.

"Are you sure?"

"Absolutely. Shady Brook Farm has lights all around the patch, and they've got a great crop this year."

"Okay. Let's do it."

I lean across the couch and grab the remote to turn the TV off. While I do that, Flynn gets up off the couch and gets his shoes and coat. I walk to my bedroom real quick and grab my black boots out of the closet, then slip them on and zip them up before I join Flynn back in the living room. I slip my phone into my pocket, then grab my wallet and keys off the table near the front door. Then I grab my coat from the coatrack.

"Okay, let's go!" Flynn says, pulling the door open.

We walk outside onto the porch and I quickly lock the door before we walk down the steps to my car. I've been driving a red AWD Honda CRV for years, and it's been my favorite car yet. It's super comfortable and it's really good in the snow. Plus, I love red because it reminds me of Christmas. Flynn and I get into the car and head to Shady Brook.

"How many pumpkins are we looking for?" Flynn asks.

"Well . . . we need at least six big ones, and then ten of different sizes."

"That's a lot of pumpkins."

"Yep. Good thing I have the wagon in the trunk," I reply.

It only takes about ten minutes to get to the farm and it's already getting dark out, but thankfully, Shady Brook does have lights around the pumpkin patch so pumpkin picking can be done later too. I'm not exactly sure how Flynn knew that considering he just came back to town—and before that he was only here for a few days during Christmas—but I'm not even going to ask him.

As soon as we get the wagon set up, I close the trunk, then lock the car. We head toward the pumpkin patch, which is down the hill from the parking lot and farm store. My family and I always loved going pumpkin picking for the house and for the B&B, and it's a tradition I make sure I keep up with.

"So how big of a pumpkin are we talking when you say big?" Flynn asks.

He clearly doesn't know me as well as he thinks.

"I'll know them when I see them," I reply.

"Wait . . . don't I get to help pick them out?"

"Nope. I'm the brains of this operation, and you're the brawn. Here, you can take the cart," I say with a giggle.

Oh, this is going to be fun.

We spend about fifteen minutes walking up and down the first three rows of the pumpkin patch, and so far, only three pumpkins jump out at me. The first is a big, perfect round shape. The second is a taller pumpkin and has the perfect stem that curves to the left, with a little curly-cue on the end. And the third doesn't really look like a circle or an oval. To me it almost looks square, so I make sure to pick that one. As we make our way down the fourth row, I find two more large, perfectly round pumpkins so I pick those up and place them in the wagon.

"This thing is getting heavy."

"I'm sure. You could always leave it here while we walk down the row."

"And leave your perfect pumpkins here? Are you crazy?"

"This is North Shore, not New York City. No one is going to steal my pumpkins if you leave them here."

"Are you sure?"

"Yep. Come walk with me?"

Flynn pulls the wagon to the side of the fourth row, then drops the handle. We begin walking up and down the fifth row, and we find a cluster of smaller pumpkins in various sizes, so we pick those up and walk them back to the wagon.

"So that's five large pumpkins, and six medium guys. Is that enough?" Flynn asks.

"Hmm, we might need a few more small guys, but I saw a bunch up in the first row. Let's head that way."

"Sounds good."

It only takes about another ten minutes and I have a wagon full of pumpkins for the B&B. Flynn and I walk side-by-side while he pulls the wagon behind us. Surprisingly, I spent less than one hundred dollars on all these pumpkins, not that I really give a shit how much it came to. I absolutely love decorating the B&B for fall and Halloween, and for winter and Christmas.

"So, do you have to take these to the B&B tonight? Or are you leaving them in your car and then heading home?" Flynn asks once we have everything loaded into the trunk.

I don't have to take these to the B&B tonight, and I'm kind of hoping that maybe he's asking because he wants to come back to the house and have dinner with me. But then again, I feel like that's tempting fate because there is clearly still a lot of passion and chemistry between us.

"I'll probably just keep them in the car for tonight, and I'll take them to work tomorrow. Why? What's up?"

"I was thinking we could go back to your house, order pizza, and finish part two of the movie. If you want to . . . "

"I would love that," I reply honestly.

We both climb into the car and a few moments later, we're driving back to my house.

I can't help but think about everything while we drive. I'm definitely the type of person who overthinks everything, and sometimes I can't help it. But I think it's about time I stop worrying about what could happen, and just let it happen. Flynn and I both agreed we are starting fresh here. We've known each other since we were kids, and we've agreed to keep what happened in the past, in the past. There is no denying the fact that we have a lot of chemistry and sexual tension between us, and quite frankly, I think I'm tired of fighting it. It was there four years ago when he came here, and it's been there every single day since he's been gone. And it's still there.

Chapter 19

Flynn

Delaney's phone has chimed a few times since we've gotten back to the house, but she hasn't actually checked her messages. If I had to guess, I would think the messages are probably coming from her brother or her best friend. Probably trying to check up on her and see how we're doing. And to be honest, everything is going fine. It's a little awkward and unsure, but fine nonetheless. After we got back from pumpkin picking, Delaney ordered the pizza and grabbed us a couple of beers, then we sat on the couch. And that's where we are right now. Waiting. I can feel the tension crackling in the air between us, and I'm relatively sure Delaney can feel it as well, but I have to make sure I keep the fact that Delaney said she wants to take things slowly in the back of my mind. The last thing I want to do is to scare her away or fuck this up.

"Can I ask you something?"

"Of course you can," Delaney replies.

I'm about to ask my question when the doorbell rings. Delaney gets up off the couch and comes back with the pizza a few minutes later. She sits a cushion away from me and puts the pizza on the coffee table.

"So, what were you going to ask?" Delaney asks, taking a slice of pizza.

"Nothing. It's not important," I reply. "Are we ready for part two of the movie?"

"Definitely!"

Delaney grabs the remote, then turns on part two of the movie. I grab a slice of pizza, then sit back and get comfortable. We're not too far into part two when I feel eyes on me. I glance to the side and Delaney is staring at me.

"What?" I ask.

"What are we doing here?"

"What are you talking about?"

"What are we doing here?" she asks again, motioning between us.

"What do you want to be doing?"

Delaney doesn't say anything and neither do I. We just stare at each other. There is so much tension you could cut it with a knife, and yes, that is a total cliché, but it's true. Out of nowhere, Delaney sets her beer on the table and leaps across the couch, into my lap.

"Delaney, I—" I begin.

"No. Just kiss me. Please."

"Please" comes out almost like a beg, and all rhyme and reason goes flying out the window, alongside with us attempting to take things slow. I slide my arms around her and slide my hands up her back as I pull her against me. We stare into each other's eyes for a few seconds before she takes control and crashes her lips against mine. I'm kind of shocked to be honest; I didn't think she would go for it first. But she did, and now I'm not sure if I'm going to be able to control myself because all that lust, emotion, and passion rushes south. I'm definitely going to try, but I'm not sure if I can do it. And apparently, Delaney isn't sure, either. She slides her arms around my neck and holds on to me as if her life depends on it. She parts her lips, then gently slides her tongue against my bottom lip. I part my lips and our tongues collide in one of the most passion-filled kisses we've ever shared. I literally feel like I'm about to unleash the beast within when Delaney stands out of nowhere.

"Are you okay? I'm sorry. I shouldn't have—"

"I'm fine," Delaney replies, taking me by the hand.

She pulls me by the hand until I stand and then she is on me again as if her life depends on it. She throws her arms around my neck and pulls me against her. I wrap my arms around her waist and lift as she wraps her legs around me and our lips collide once again. We kiss feverishly as I slowly walk us toward the bedroom. I get just outside her bedroom door when I'm hit with an awful case of déjà vu. I stop walking and pull my face from Delaney's. She's panting and she looks confused.

"Delaney . . . I have to ask. Are you absolutely sure you want to do this now?"

I need to make sure I ask her and get an answer because once I start, I know I'm not going to be able to stop. I'm already rock-hard and the only thing I can think about right now is getting Delaney into her bed and naked beneath me.

"Don't you want me?" she asks in an upset tone.

I brush her hair from her face and gently kiss her lips before I pull back. "Of course I want you, Delaney. I've wanted you every day for the last four years. But I know you said you want to take things slow, and I don't want to hurt or upset you. I have to ask you again. Are you sure you want to do this right now?"

Delaney doesn't answer right away, and I wonder if maybe she's changing her mind now that she has a moment to think.

"Flynn, I am so crazy in love with you, and I have been since we were freaking kids. I don't care how we got here . . . the point is, we did. And I want you. I wanted you then, and I want you now. So badly."

That's all I need to hear. My lips are on Delaney's in a second, and I cross the threshold into her bedroom as quickly and carefully as possible. I gently place her down once we get near the bed and stare down into her beautiful eyes.

"I love you too, Delaney. I always have."

And that is the absolute truth. I have loved this woman for so long, and I am ridiculously excited and happy to be where I am with her right now.

Delaney looks up at me, and I can see the desire and passion written all over her face and in her eyes. She moves her hands to the bottom of her shirt and begins to pull it up, but I stop her. She looks shocked. But after what happened last time, I should be the one to stand before her. I lean down and gently kiss Delaney's lips, then I take a step back and pull off my shirt. I unbutton my jeans, then push them down and kick them off to the side. Delaney's eyes travel up and down my body and if possible her eyes turn even more seductive. I should feel vulnerable right now, as I'm standing here in my boxers, but the desire of the moment has me feeling nothing but absolute lust for this woman.

I'm about to push down my boxers when Delaney quickly lifts her shirt off and tosses it to the floor. Then she unbuttons her jeans and slides them down her legs. She quickly kicks them off to the side, then looks up at me with what can only be described as 'fuck me' eyes before she sucks her bottom lip in between her teeth. It's a move that makes me want to pounce—yes, literally pounce—but I do my best to control myself.

I step toward Delaney, then reach around her and quickly unfasten her bra, letting it fall to the floor. Her beautiful breasts fall free, and the sight goes straight to my dick. I get even harder, if that's at all possible.

"Fuck."

I kind of want to face-palm myself right now. Of all the things I could possibly say in this moment, that's the only thing that comes out of my mouth.

"Is that a good fuck or a bad fuck?" Delaney asks with a grin.

Cheeky shit.

I take a step forward so Delaney and I are chest to chest again. I slide my hands onto her hips, and she slides her hands up my chest and settles them on my arms.

"It's a good fuck, sweetheart. Believe me. You are even more beautiful than I remember."

Delaney smiles, and I swear I see a slight blush appear on her adorable cheeks.

My god do I love this woman. Probably more than she'll ever realize.

"I bet you say that to all the girls."

So freaking sassy...

"Nope, just you. Always you," I reply as I slip her panties down.

***

Delaney

This is it. This is the moment I have been waiting for. I wanted to take things slowly, but then it finally hit me that time is short, and tomorrow is never a guarantee. If I was going to do this, then it was going to happen now. So I went for it. When I jumped into Flynn's lap, I could instantly feel his arousal against my ass. And that, of course, turned me on even more. We made it into the hallway outside my room in a flash, but then when Flynn stopped and asked me if I was sure, I was actually taken aback for a moment. This man is completely different from the man I met four years ago. Everything feels completely different now, and I know that's because there are no secrets between us. It is just passion . . . and love.

I slide my hands down Flynn's arms and settle them on the waistband of his boxers. I look up at him and lightly lick my lip, then slide his boxers down and allow his hard cock to spring free.

I swear it's like an evil, horny beast takes over my body, and I'm suddenly unable to control myself. I wrap my hand around his cock and lightly lick the head a few times before I glance up at him. I can see the desire written all over his gorgeous face, and I know that it's time. I want to taste him—like, *really* taste him.

Little by little, I slide his cock into my mouth. I go until I feel him in the back of my throat, then I pull back and do the same thing again, and again, and again. The noises that are coming out of Flynn's mouth just egg me on further, and I love the power and control I have right now. I've had sex before, but it was always very vanilla and quick. Looking up at Flynn's gorgeous body, I know I don't want this to be quick. I want to take my time savoring his gorgeous cock, and then I want to take him by the hand and lead him to the bed before we do unspeakable things to one another. And I want it to happen again and again. All. Fucking. Night.

Flynn slides as hands through my hair, then pushes my head gently. His cock hits the back of my throat, and I start to gag a little bit, though it doesn't bother me. I find it hot as fuck, and it turns me on even more. I begin bobbing my head up and down faster and faster, and I feel like a sex-crazed beast.

"Oh, fuck," Flynn groans.

I look up at him and he's looking down at me like he wants to devour me. I pull back and smile up at him, and I'm about to quite literally swallow his cock again when he stops me. In the fastest move known to man, Flynn leans down and picks me up and tosses me onto the bed. I bounce a little, which makes my tits bounce, and Flynn's eyes never leave my body. He stands at the foot of the bed, staring at me like he is about to do unthinkable, dirty things to me, and I love every second of it.

He climbs onto the bed and hovers over me. Holding himself up with his glorious, muscular arms. He leans down and gently kisses my lips, then positions himself between my thighs. He leans down and guides his cock toward my entrance, and I shudder the moment I feel him run the head of his cock from my entrance to my clit and back again.

"Mmm," I moan softly.

"So wet already," Flynn growls.

"Always for you," I whisper.

"I love you, Delaney."

"I love you too, Flynn."

And with that, Flynn slowly begins to thrust. His cock feels amazing the second it slides into me, and I swear I see stars. He goes slowly, giving me time to get used to his size, but slow isn't working for me.

"Faster, Flynn. Please."

And he listens. He begins thrusting faster, going deeper with each thrust. If I thought I saw stars before, I was wrong. He hits spots that haven't been hit in so fucking long, and I can already feel my orgasm beginning to build.

"Oh god, babe, you feel amazing," Flynn groans.

"You. Do. Too," I manage to get out in between my heavy breathing.

Flynn lowers onto me, and he takes my hands in his and holds them above my head while he thrusts into me. I wrap my legs around him and use my feet to tap his ass every time he thrusts. He gently kisses my lips, but the kiss turns wild the moment our tongues collide. Flynn lets go of my hands, and I immediately slide them around his neck, then he slides his hands on either side of my head. I can feel him pulsing inside me, and I know his orgasm is coming quickly too. I try to hold off, but I'm having a very hard time keeping it in. Flynn leans back a little and slides his hand down to my clit. He slowly rubs while he thrusts in and out. The motion of what he's doing has me moaning and groaning more than I ever have, and I know I'm seconds from having a massive orgasm.

"Not yet, Delaney," Flynn groans when he pulls back.

I start to feel super sensitive and warm all over, and I know that I'm about to lose it. I know Flynn is really close too because he begins thrusting harder and harder. I open my mouth to speak, but I am unable to get any words out. The warm feeling takes over and spreads throughout my body, and my eyes roll back into my head as my orgasm slams into me, which then sends Flynn over the edge.

"Fuck!" he roars as he collapses on top of me.

"Holy . . . fuck . . . That was . . . amazing," I pant.

Flynn gently pulls out, then moves over so he's lying next to me. He pulls me against his chest and holds me while we both struggle to catch our breath.

"You're amazing. I'm never . . . letting you go," Flynn says in between deep breaths.

"Sounds good to me."

"Delaney . . . I need to ask you something. And it's important," Flynn says seriously.

Uh-oh. Please don't let something bad happen again.

"What's up?" I ask, concerned.

"Will you be my girlfriend?" he asks with a huge grin.

I can't help but chuckle—not because it's a silly thing, but because it's incredibly cute. If I'm being completely honest, it was totally unexpected in this moment.

"Of course I'll be your girlfriend."

"Okay, good," Flynn says with a huge grin.

Chapter 20

Delaney

I wake up the next morning feeling absolutely incredible. A little sore, but incredible. Flynn and I ended up having sex three times last night, plus we stayed up talking for a while, which was also incredible. The man I've gotten to know over the last twenty-four hours is a completely different man than I knew four years ago. I could see us dating and having fun. I could see us getting engaged and getting married eventually. I could even see us having kids together. I could definitely see myself spending the rest of my life with him.

"Whatcha thinking about?" Flynn asks.

"Hey. I thought you were still asleep," I reply, surprised.

He was literally just softly sawing down the forest, so I'm pretty surprised that he's suddenly awake.

"I was, but I woke up and the bed was empty next to me. I thought you left me," he says dramatically.

"Oh brother," I reply, rolling my eyes.

Flynn laughs, then walks across the kitchen and stands behind me at the island. He wraps his arms around me, leans down, and gently kisses my neck.

"Everything okay, babe?"

"Yes, everything is perfect. I have to get the pumpkins over to the B&B this morning, so I figured I would get showered and dressed, then come out here and start the coffee."

"Ah. I forgot about the pumpkins."

"Yep. Plus, Joy and I are meeting for a coffee catch-up after I take the pumpkins to the B&B."

"Very nice," Flynn replies.

"Yep. Love our coffee catch-ups. Should be fun."

"Are you going to tell her all the steamy details about how I—" he begins as he leans down and kisses my neck again.

"Flynn," I warn.

"And how I—"

"Flynn!"

"I'm just kidding. Do you mind if I hang out here for the day?" he asks with a chuckle.

"No, that's fine."

"Okay. Dylan said something about me maybe coming by to help him today, but he wasn't sure. Said he would let me know."

"That'll be fun."

"Yep. When are you leaving?"

"In about five seconds," I reply.

"Okay. I'll see you later then?"

"Maybeeeee," I reply in a sassy tone.

Before I can say another word, Flynn scoops me up off the stool.

"Put me down!" I squeal.

"Nope. Not until you agree to come home and have dinner with me . . . and then have some more mind-blowing sex tonight."

"Well, duh," I reply.

Flynn lets out a deep laugh, then sets me down and wraps his arms around me, pulling me against his chest. I manage to get my arms out from my sides and wrap them around him, hugging him tightly. Last night meant everything to me and I am very much looking forward to seeing where life takes us in the future.

"Love you, babe," Flynn says, pulling me from my thoughts.

I look up at his beautiful brown eyes and smile. "I love you too."

Flynn leans down and gently places his lips onto mine. This kiss is not as sex-crazed as last night's kisses, but it's just as passionate. We stand there and make out like teenagers for a few minutes, and when we pull back, I am completely flustered and breathless.

"I have to go. I'll see you later."

"Yes, you definitely will," Flynn replies with a wink.

I give Flynn a hug and lean up and gently kiss his lips before turning around to walk away. Flynn leans forward and smacks my ass as I walk away, and I can't help but squeal. He gives me a wink, then heads back down the hall into my bedroom. *My goodness, does he look all sexy and steamy walking through my house in nothing but boxers and sex hair. I could definitely get used to it.*

I quickly slip on my boots and jacket, then grab my keys and wallet off the entryway table. As I pull my front door open, a chilly blast of air hits me, and I can't help but shiver. It definitely feels much chillier than yesterday.

I make my way to the car, then climb in and get it started. I let it run for a few minutes before I pull out of the driveway and head to the B&B. A few minutes later, I pull into the B&B's employee parking lot.

Dylan said he would be waiting for me to gather the pumpkins, and the B&B is not far from the coffee shop, so I decide to leave my car at the B&B and walk to meet Joy.

Ten minutes later, I've got my coffee and our table, and I'm waiting for Joy to get there. Not even five minutes after I sit down, Joy comes flying into the coffee shop. She completely passes the counter and comes right to the table and sits with wide eyes.

"Tell me everything!"

"Jesus, Joy. Don't you want to get your coffee first?"

"Nope! Dish. Now!"

Joy never was very patient when it came to getting some juicy gossip, so I start at the beginning and tell her everything. I leave nothing out. Well . . . I might leave some of the sexual things out, but that's because Flynn and I do deserve to have some privacy.

"Oh my god, Delaney! So, are you guys officially an item? Are you going to keep seeing each other? Is he here for good?"

"Good lord, Joy. Calm down! Yes, we are officially an item. Yes, we are going to keep seeing each other. And yes, he is here for good."

I'm expecting Joy to smile and laugh and say a lot of encouraging words and genuinely be happy for me. But what I'm not expecting is the sudden squeal she lets out. It's loud and she actually scares the crap out of me.

"I'm so fucking happy for you, Del!"

"Thank you," I reply with a huge grin.

Truth be told, I'm really fucking excited myself. I never—not in my wildest dreams—thought Finn and I would find our way back to one another after what happened four years ago. I guess you could say I have to thank my brother, because if he hadn't come home to take over the B&B, then Flynn probably never would've come back here. And then we never would've reconnected. And then there's also the fact that Joy and Dylan both talked some sense into me. I definitely owe them everything.

"So, what happens now?" Joy asks.

"What do you mean?"

"I mean . . . you had sex already. Are you guys going to casually date? Are you going to be exclusive? Are you going to move in together?"

"Whoa. Easy, girl!" I chuckle and take a sip of my coffee. "I don't know what's going to happen, but I know what I want to happen. I can't say whether or not that's exactly what's going to happen."

"Okay. Strictly between us, what do you want to happen?"

"I want us to date and see how it goes and stay together. If I'm being one-hundred percent completely honest, I could see myself marrying Flynn and having kids with him."

"That is so fucking cute. Do you think he feels the same?"

"Oh, he definitely feels the same," a voice says a few feet away.

I look up with wide eyes and see Flynn standing near the door with Dylan. Joy turns around, then looks back at me with the same wide eyes.

Oops.

"Uh . . . hi, guys. What's up?" I ask, totally changing the subject.

Dylan and Flynn walk toward the table and Flynn bends down to give me a kiss the moment he reaches me. Not going to lie, I get butterflies in my stomach the moment he does that. Clearly, he's not afraid to show affection in front of my brother, or in front of other people.

"Nothing. We wanted to come by and grab coffees before we go back to the B&B to do pumpkin placement for this incredibly annoying innkeeper and her decorating OCD," Flynn replies with a smile.

"Oh, shit," Joy whispers.

"On that note, I'm going to order my coffee. Later, sis," Dylan says before he scurries away.

"I think I need a refill," Joy says before she jumps up out of her chair and goes to join Dylan at the counter.

I can't help but roll my eyes. Especially since Joy doesn't even have a cup yet.

Oy.

Flynn looks at me and gives me a big smile, then he leans down and kisses me again. "You know I'm just fucking with you."

"No, you're not," I reply.

"Nope. I'm not."

"You're lucky you're cute," I reply.

"True story," he says with a huge grin.

Dylan walks back to the table, then hands Flynn his coffee. "Okay, shit-bag. Let's go. See ya later, sis."

"Bye, babe." Flynn leans down and kisses me for a third time.

Ah, more butterflies!

Dylan and Flynn walk out, and I can't help but shake my head while smiling.

"You love him," Joy says in a teasing tone when she sits back down.

"Shut up."

"In all seriousness, Del, I am super excited and happy for you. You deserve to be so fucking happy."

"Thank you, Joy."

"Plus, now we can go out for double-date nights!" she squeals with a huge smile.

"Yes, I guess we can."

"Woo-hoo," Joy says loudly.

"Shh."

"Never."

We laugh, then continue to drink our coffees and talk. I look forward to our coffee catch-up dates every week, but I never have much to report. I'd be lying if I said I wasn't excited to finally have something to talk about.

Epilogue

Delaney | One Year Later

The last year has been absolutely amazing. Dylan and I talked and decided to become co-innkeepers at the B&B, with Flynn coming on as manager. Figuring out how we worked together as a trio took a few weeks, but once we had it down, we were a pretty awesome team. My parents were so impressed that they decided to fully retire and move to southern South Carolina. They planned to sell their house, but decided to find out if one of us wanted it first. Dylan and I talked and we both decided I would take the house, so I sold my place and moved into the family home.

Flynn stayed with Dylan for the first four months after he came back to North Shore, but we got pretty serious pretty quickly and decided it was time for him to move in with me. He packed up his stuff and moved into my home a month after Mom and Dad moved down south.

I look back at everything that has happened in the last few years, and I can't believe that this is my life now. Not only am I with the man of my dreams, but everything else is looking up as well. The B&B is doing amazing, and we're busier than ever. Joy and her husband are also doing amazing, and they're actually expecting their first little girl. I'm super excited to be an auntie, and I told them I would babysit whenever they needed someone.

My phone suddenly chimes, so I grab it and see a message from Joy.

Hey, lady. How's it going? How was your day today?

It's going just fine. Was a nice day today. What are you doing up?

Your niece doesn't like sleep. This is just the beginning. I'm doomed.

You're not doomed. You're just going to be really tired. Maybe I should buy you a new coffee maker for your birthday?

Ha. Ha. Ha. And also, yes please. *winky face*

smiley face You know you love me. And done!

Yeah, whatever. Also, woo-hoo! *smiley face* What are you guys doing for your anniversary tomorrow?

We're going to the B&B for brunch, then Flynn wanted to take a walk by the lake afterward.

Omg, do you think he's going to propose?

I don't know, but I want him to.

I have no idea to be honest. Both him and my brother are TERRIBLE at keeping secrets, and neither of them have been acting weird or anything. Maybe he isn't ready yet.

Are you?

To get engaged to the man who has had my heart since I was thirteen? Of course I am. But it'll happen when it's meant to happen.

It's crazy to think I've been in love with Flynn since I was a young teenager. What kid knows what love is? I certainly shouldn't have. But I did. I knew that what I felt was more than friendship. I knew it then, and I still know it.

"Hey, gorgeous. Whatcha thinking about?" Flynn asks as he walks into the living room.

"Oh, nothing. Just thinking about how happy I am."

And it's true. Nothing could make me happier than how I'm feeling right now. Well . . . something could, but I'm not ready for that just yet. Maybe next year.

"Happy, huh? Why's that?"

"Shut up, shithead," I reply with a giggle.

Flynn let's out a deep laugh, then plops down on the couch next to me.

Tomorrow is our one-year anniversary and we're planning on going to the B&B for a 'special anniversary brunch.' Flynn's words, not mine.

"Don't you think we should get to bed so we're well-rested for tomorrow?"

"Oh, relax, old man. We can stay up a little longer," I reply with a smile.

"Old man?"

I keep my eyes focused on the TV, but I can feel Flynn's gaze burning a hole into the side of my head.

"Can I help you?" I ask, glancing to the side.

"Old man, my ass," he mutters, tickling the hell out of me.

"Oh my god! Okay, stop. I'm sorry!" I blurt out when I can't stand the tickling anymore.

"I knew you'd surrender," Flynn says and stands. "Shall we?"

I grab the remote and turn the TV off, then take Flynn's hand. We walk upstairs and down the hallway to our bedroom, like we've done before. Only this time, the door is closed, and Flynn stops me before I walk inside.

"Would you be upset if we don't go to the B&B for brunch tomorrow?"

Oh . . .

"No. Why would I be?"

I try to hide the disappointment that he probably isn't going to propose, but Flynn knows me better than many and knows I'm lying.

"What is it, hon?"

"Nothing. I'm getting sleepy. Why don't we head to bed?"

"Sure. After you, babe," Flynn says, stepping aside.

I turn the doorknob and push the door open, and my heart literally drops into my stomach.

Oh. My. God.

There are candles lit on both of our dressers and there is a path of red rose petals that leads from the door to the bed. Each nightstand contains a vase of sunflowers and red roses—which are my two favorite flowers.

I enter the room and walk until I am standing at the foot of the bed. On the bed in red rose pedals is a heart shape and in the very center of the heart is a closed ring box. I already can't hold back the tears that are forming and rolling down my cheeks. I turn around and Flynn stands with me at the foot of the bed. He leans over and grabs the box and turns back to face me.

"Flynn . . . I—" I begin, but I get all choked up and can't form the words.

Without warning, Flynn drops to one knee then looks up at me.

This is it. Oh my god.

"Delaney, you are everything I've ever wanted in a partner. You're beautiful, smart, caring, forgiving, and have the purest heart of anyone I've ever met. When I first came back into your life five years ago, I did everything wrong. I lied and I broke your trust, and though I did not deserve a second chance with you, your pure, loving heart allowed you to forgive me and give me a second chance. And I will be forever grateful that you gave me that opportunity. Over the last year, I've learned there is not a single thing I don't love about you. I'm sure there is much more to learn about you, and I want to spend the rest of my life doing so. Delaney Marie Williams, will you marry me?"

If you've ever watched a romantic movie and the guy proposes, the woman always looks emotional, but beautiful and put-together. That is not me, not in the slightest. Right now, I have tears pouring down my face and I can barely see. I quickly use my sleeves to wipe my eyes—and nonchalantly wipe my nose—then stare down at this gorgeous man who will always have my heart. I take a deep breath and smile.

"Yes, I'll marry you, Flynn. A thousand times yes!"

Flynn stands and pulls me into a hug, then leans down and gently kisses me. I stand on my tippy-toes and wrap my arms around his neck and enjoy my first kiss with my fiancé. We pull apart, breathless. Breathless, but smiling massive smiles. Flynn takes the ring out of the box and slips it on my finger. He definitely did his research because the ring not only fits perfectly but also is absolutely gorgeous.

"Did I do good?"

"It's gorgeous," I whisper.

"I saw the way your eyes lit up when we saw it in that little store down in South Carolina when we visited your folks a few weeks ago. I knew that that was the one."

"You . . . did really . . . good," I say in between crying and trying to breathe.

Flynn leans down and presses his lips against mine and kisses me with the passion I hope we share forever. He pulls back, then smiles down at me.

"I love you so much, Delaney."

"I love you, too, Flynn. Always and forever."

The End

About the Author

A.M. Olenick is an avid reader turned author writing contemporary romance and paranormal romance. Her stories range from sweet to steamy & everything in between. In her world, you can find sexy alpha-type men, vampires, and shifters alongside smart & sassy heroines who always get the happy endings that they deserve. She was born & raised in New Jersey, where she still resides with her family. She's a hopeless romantic, a boy mom, a dog mom, a coffee-o-holic, and a lover of tattoos, the beach, sunflowers and roses, and all things Christmas.

Join A.M. Olenick Online:

Official Website:

www.amolenickwrites.com

Facebook:

A.M. Olenick

Instagram:
author.am.olenick

TikTok:
author.am.olenick

Made in the USA
Monee, IL
08 September 2022

13541265R00083